THE ALPHA'S CHRISTMAS WISH

HOBSON HILLS OMEGAS: BOOK SEVEN

C.W. GRAY

Thank you for visiting the world of Hobson Hills Omegas. I love this series and appreciate each and every one of you that read it. Below, I've included a few family trees made by the wonderful Missy Schwarz. The family trees for books three and four are particularly useful for this book.

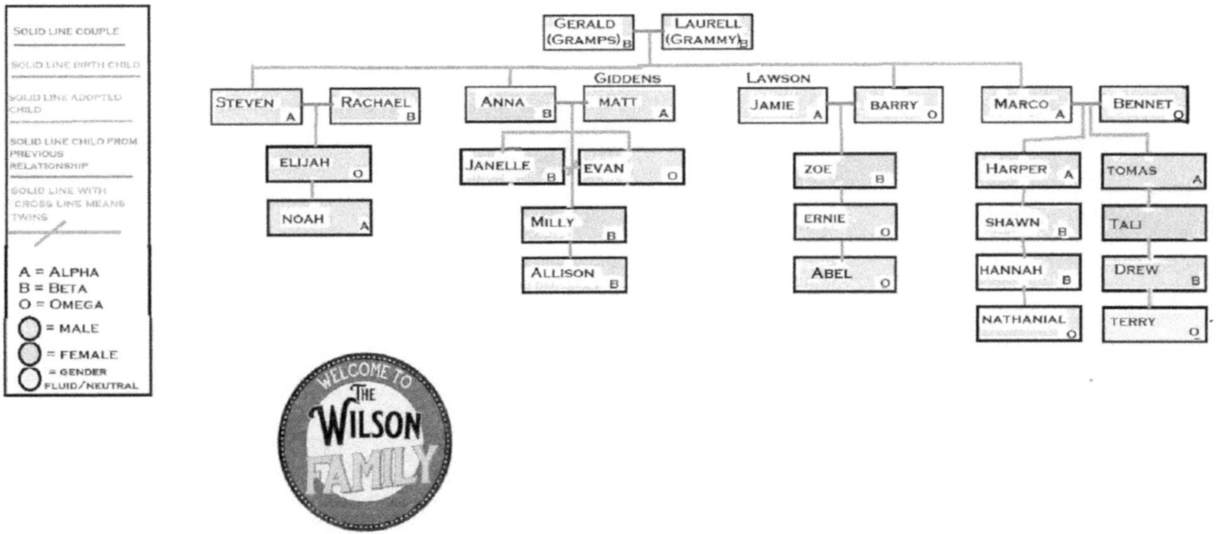

The Wilson Family Tree

GERALD (GRAMPS) B — LAURELL (GRAMMY) B

Steven A — Rachael B
- Elijah O
- Noah A

Giddens — Anna B — Matt A
- Janelle B — Evan O
- Milly B
- Allison B

Lawson — Jamie A — Barry O
- Zoe B
- Ernie O
- Abel O

Marco A — Bennet O
- Harper A — Tomas A
- Shawn B — Tali
- Hannah B — Drew B
- Nathanial O — Terry O

Legend

- SOLID LINE COUPLE
- SOLID LINE BIRTH CHILD
- SOLID LINE ADOPTED CHILD
- SOLID LINE CHILD FROM PREVIOUS RELATIONSHIP
- SOLID LINE WITH CROSS LINE MEANS TWINS

- A = ALPHA
- B = BETA
- O = OMEGA

- ◯ = MALE
- ◯ = FEMALE
- ◯ = GENDER FLUID/NEUTRAL

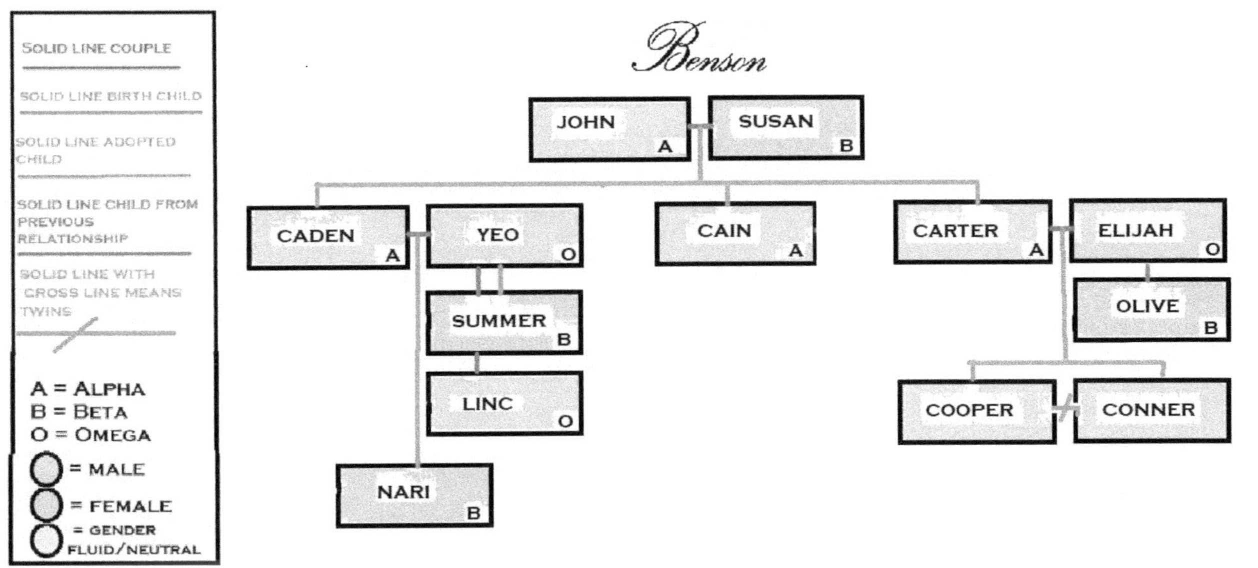

Benson
JOHN A
SUSAN B
CADEN A
YEO O
CAIN A
CARTER A
ELIJAH O
SUMMER B
OLIVE B
LINC O
COOPER
CONNER
NARI B
SOLID LINE COUPLE
SOLID LINE BIRTH CHILD
SOLID LINE ADOPTED CHILD
SOLID LINE CHILD FROM PREVIOUS RELATIONSHIP
SOLID LINE WITH CROSS LINE MEANS TWINS
A = ALPHA
B = BETA
O = OMEGA
= MALE
= FEMALE
= GENDER FLUID/NEUTRAL

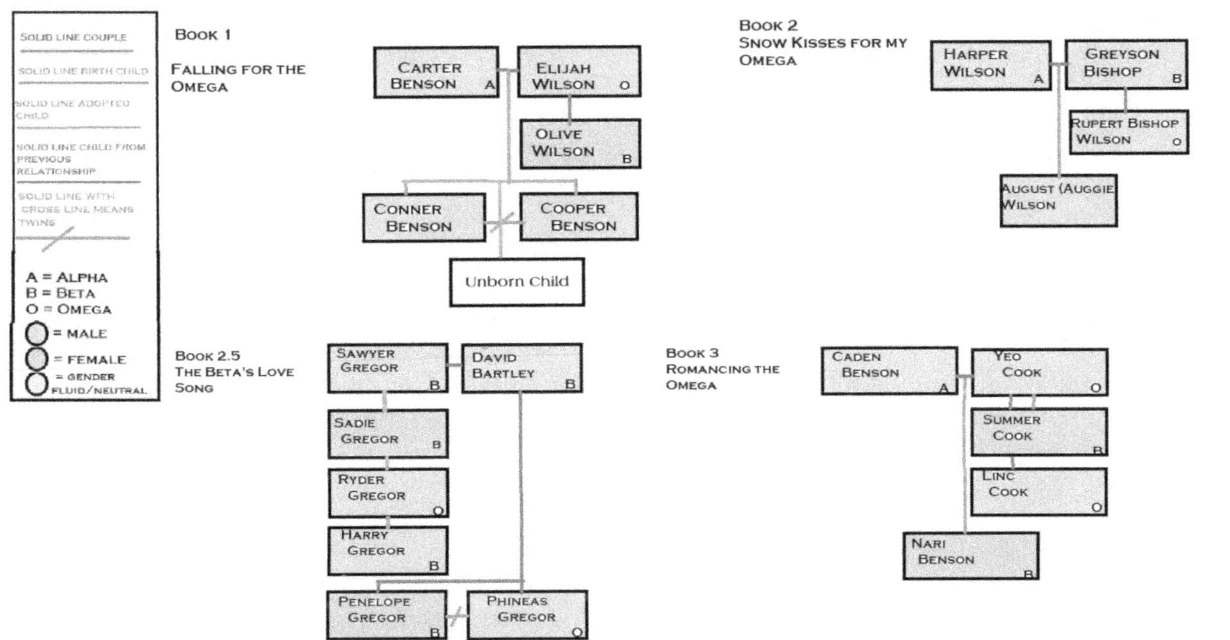

SOLID LINE COUPLE
SOLID LINE BIRTH CHILD
SOLID LINE ADOPTED CHILD
SOLID LINE CHILD FROM PREVIOUS RELATIONSHIP
SOLID LINE WITH CROSS LINE MEANS TWINS
A = ALPHA
B = BETA
O = OMEGA
= MALE
= FEMALE
= GENDER FLUID/NEUTRAL
Book 1
FALLING FOR THE OMEGA
CARTER BENSON A
ELIJAH WILSON O
OLIVE WILSON B
CONNER BENSON
COOPER BENSON
Unborn Child
Book 2
SNOW KISSES FOR MY OMEGA
HARPER WILSON A
GREYSON BISHOP B
RUPERT BISHOP WILSON O
AUGUST (AUGGIE WILSON
Book 2.5
THE BETA'S LOVE SONG
SAWYER GREGOR B
DAVID BARTLEY B
SADIE GREGOR B
RYDER GREGOR O
HARRY GREGOR B
PENELOPE GREGOR B
PHINEAS GREGOR O
Book 3
ROMANCING THE OMEGA
CADEN BENSON A
YEO COOK O
SUMMER COOK B
LINC COOK O
NARI BENSON B

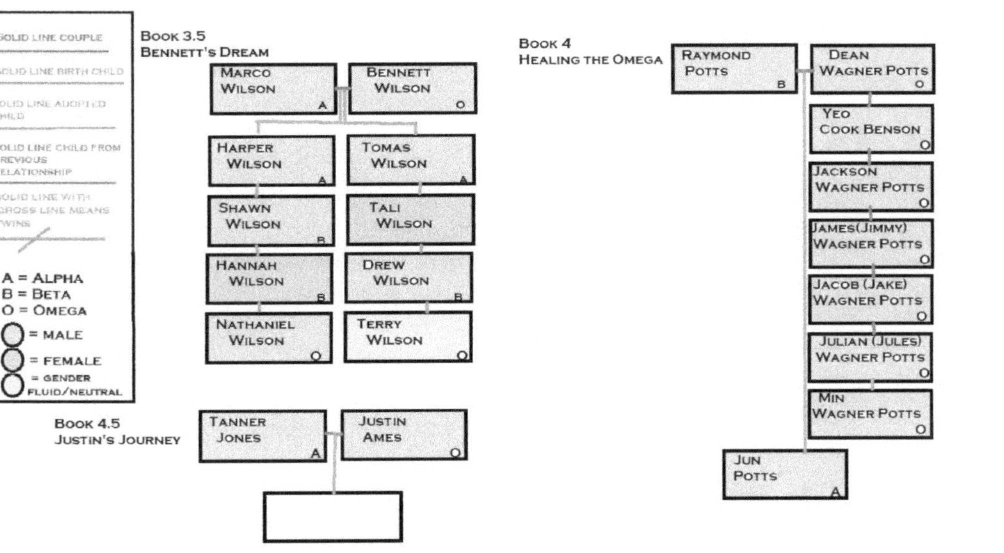

Solid line couple
Solid line birth child
Solid line adopted child
Solid line child from previous relationship
Solid line with cross line means twins
A = Alpha
B = Beta
O = Omega
= Male
= Female
= Gender fluid/neutral
Book 3.5
Bennett's Dream
Marco Wilson A
Bennett Wilson O
Harper Wilson A
Tomas Wilson A
Shawn Wilson B
Tali Wilson
Hannah Wilson B
Drew Wilson B
Nathaniel Wilson O
Terry Wilson O
Book 4.5
Justin's Journey
Tanner Jones A
Justin Ames O
Book 4
Healing the Omega
Raymond Potts B
Dean Wagner Potts O
Yeo Cook Benson O
Jackson Wagner Potts O
James(Jimmy) Wagner Potts O
Jacob (Jake) Wagner Potts O
Julian (Jules) Wagner Potts O
Min Wagner Potts O
Jun Potts A

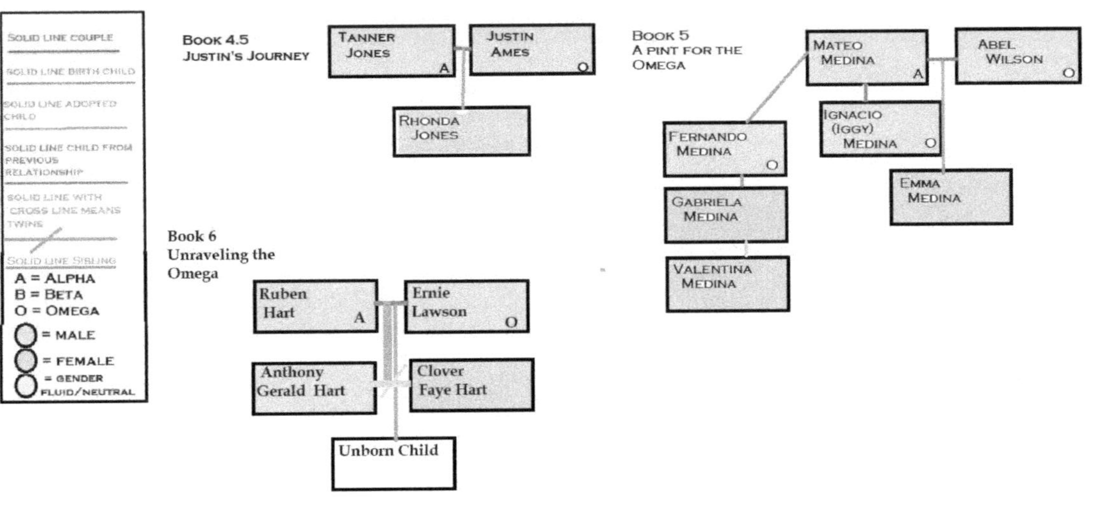

SOLID LINE COUPLE
SOLID LINE BIRTH CHILD
SOLID LINE ADOPTED CHILD
SOLID LINE CHILD FROM PREVIOUS RELATIONSHIP
SOLID LINE WITH CROSS LINE MEANS TWINS
SOLID LINE SIBLING
A = ALPHA
B = BETA
O = OMEGA
= MALE
= FEMALE
= GENDER FLUID/NEUTRAL
BOOK 4.5
JUSTIN'S JOURNEY
TANNER JONES
A
JUSTIN AMES
O
RHONDA JONES
Book 6
Unraveling the Omega
Ruben Hart
A
Ernie Lawson
O
Anthony Gerald Hart
Clover Faye Hart
Unborn Child
BOOK 5
A PINT FOR THE OMEGA
MATEO MEDINA
A
ABEL WILSON
O
IGNACIO (IGGY) MEDINA
O
FERNANDO MEDINA
O
EMMA MEDINA
GABRIELA MEDINA
VALENTINA MEDINA

Supporting Families

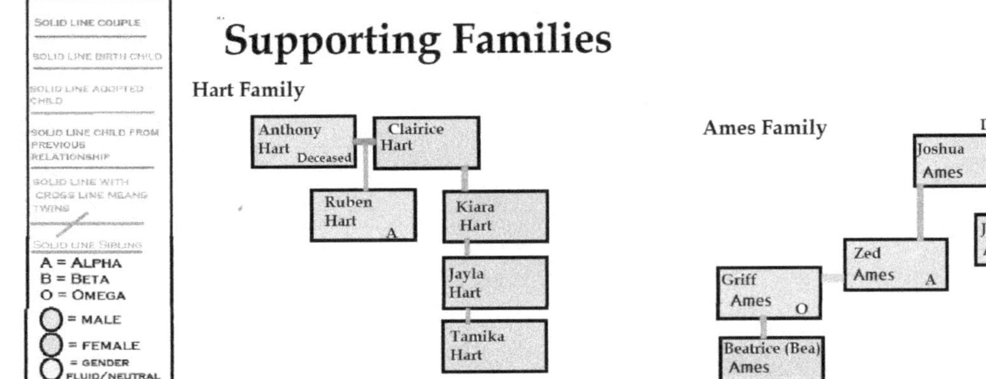

CHAPTER 1

JUAN

Juan Vega balanced on the bottom of the extension ladder and pulled the hose of his nail gun around to his other side. "It's fucking freezing out here. Why the hell are we working outside today?"

His friend Tomás laughed. "Because it's for Ernie."

Juan cursed under his breath. Tomás was right. It may be fucking winter in Maine, but Reuben wanted Ernie to have his own knitting room. They had finished the inside a few days ago. All that was left was nailing the wood siding onto the new addition. Fortunately, they were almost finished.

Something tugged on the bottom of his jacket, and he looked down. Peppermint, Reuben's alpaca, watched him while he munched on the cloth. The silly thing wore a bright red, knitted Christmas hat and scarf.

"Why is the alpaca in the backyard?" Tomás asked, laughing.

"Ernie told me Reuben worried the other alpacas

were picking on Peppermint, so Peppermint gets to stay in the backyard for part of the day," Juan said, shaking his head. The man was full of shit. He just wanted his damn alpaca closer to him.

Tomás chuckled. "Hurry up, and let's get this shit done. Ernie has coffee inside."

Juan shook his hips, but Peppermint held on to his coat. He sighed and ignored the alpaca while they finished the siding.

He stepped off the ladder, and the backdoor opened. Pudge, Ernie's puppy, barked and ran outside, hopping through the snow to reach them.

"It looks good, guys," Ernie said, waving at them as he yawned. "I have coffee and some of Reuben's gingerbread cookies inside."

Juan and Tomás cleaned up their tools and extracted Juan's coat from Peppermint. Juan kicked the snow from his boots before going inside. "Damn, it's cold."

"You've been here three years, Juan," Ernie said, snorting. "You only get to complain about the cold the first year."

Juan mock scowled at his friend as he took off his heavy coat and gloves. "Just give me some damn cookies and one of those babies."

Ernie chuckled and picked up Tony from the infant rocker. Juan took the baby and swayed. *Damn, I want one of these.* Green eyes and a freckled face with Korean features filled his mind. *Damn, I want one of these with Jackson.*

Ernie handed Tomás Clover, Tony's twin sister,

then waved them to the table. "Sit down, and I'll get you some cookies and coffee. Juan, when's the next excursion? Mateo and Artie are in, so Carter and Noah can have a break for the night."

Juan frowned. "How much experience does Mateo have? Artie can carry the bags, but we need someone to work the equipment."

Ernie set a plate of gingerbread men between Juan and Tomás. "He's good for it. We'll find Bigfoot this time. I know it."

Juan ate his cookies and cuddled Tony while they talked. Ernie was a good guy, even if he was a little strange. When Juan moved to Hobson Hills about three years ago, the omega had become one of his closest friends.

"Okay, before you two go, I made you guys something." Ernie stood and grabbed a box off the counter. "Reuben and I really appreciate you two jumping into this project so quickly. Having a knitting room lets me keep all my stuff. I was going to have to either pile it in the bedroom or give it away."

Juan couldn't imagine Ernie not knitting. "We don't mind, Red."

Ernie smiled and pulled out a dark green, knitted cable sweater. "This one is for you, Tomás. It makes your eyes pop. Here's a matching scarf to go with it."

Tomás smiled and took his gifts. "Thanks, Ernie."

Ernie bent and hugged him. "That's what cousins are for."

Juan hid his smile at Tomás's blush. After a

childhood spent having no one, Tomás adored having a large extended family.

"For you, Juan, we have a cream sweater." Ernie pulled out a thick, cream, cable-knit sweater. "I made it to match your green fauxhawk, then you went and colored your damn hair."

Juan ran a hand through his black hair. "It's time I become a mature adult, Red."

Ernie pouted and stomped his foot. "I miss the green."

Juan took his sweater and set it aside. "I kinda do too. Maybe it'll be green again after Christmas."

A little while later, Juan said goodbye to Ernie and Tomás. He had an emergency patching job to do at Bennett and Marco's house. As soon as he pulled out of Ernie's driveway, his phone rang. He saw the number and smiled. "Hey, Papa."

"Juan, I hate to interrupt you while you're working," said Juan's omega dad, Eduardo.

"You know you can call anytime, Papa," Juan said. He loved his papa, but he knew he didn't call unless there was a good reason.

Juan had been close to his papa when he was a child, but Jorge Vega didn't want his alpha son to spend too much time with his omega father. Juan's alpha dad was a dick, but that didn't stop Juan from following the man's wishes anyway.

"Lucía is getting married," Eduardo said. Juan could hear the happiness in his voice. "Manuel is a fine young man."

"I refuse to believe it," Juan said, grinning. "I'm still

having trouble remembering she's not a skinny ten-year-old anymore."

"She's twenty-two," Eduardo said dryly. "Your dad has been on her for years to find a nice man and settle down."

Juan laughed. Lucía had refused to fit into the *little lady* box their alpha dad had built for her. She had refused to marry the first boy who proposed and had graduated top of her college class. Now, she worked for a marketing firm and made more than their dad.

"I'm happy for her. When's the wedding?"

"This summer," Eduardo answered. "I'll get you the exact dates as soon as she pays for the venue. Now, tell me how your day has been?"

"I finished Ernie's addition," he said. "Now I'm on the way to a friend's house to patch a wall."

"Ernie? Oh, he's that omega friend of yours," Eduardo said. "Oh, your dad wants the phone."

Jorge's strong voice came across the line. "Did you finally man up and get that omega in bed?"

Juan wrinkled his nose. "Dad, I told you Ernie and I are just friends."

"Alphas and omegas can't be friends, son," Jorge said, scoffing. "An alpha has needs, and omegas need to be taken care of. That's what we're made for. It's not right for you to be thirty-four and still single. You need to settle down."

Juan almost disconnected his Bluetooth, but he knew his dad would just call back.

"If you go on treating omegas like they're your buddy, you're never going to get married," Jorge continued. "You'll be cooking your own dinner for the rest of your life."

"Okay, Dad," Juan said and pulled into Bennett's driveway. He didn't agree with his alpha dad, but it was easier to just go along with him sometimes. "I need to get back to work."

"Remember what I said," Jorge said and hung up the phone.

Juan parked and leaned his head back. His dad thought alphas needed to be dominant, loud, and demanding. Juan had to admit he was kind of loud, but he preferred nice and easy most of the time. He'd had more than enough of dominant and aggressive idiots in the army. Fuck, he'd lost some good friends because of one particularly aggressive alpha colonel.

A knock on his window made him open his eyes. Bennett stood outside, all bundled up. His youngest son, Nate, was perched on his hip. "You okay in there?"

Juan grinned and pushed his depressing thoughts away. He'd save those for later when he was trying to sleep. "Yeah, just taking a short nap."

He got out of the car and grabbed his tools before following Bennett inside.

"You need to get more sleep," Bennett said, eyeing him. "I see those bags under your eyes, young man."

Juan shrugged and kept grinning. "No rest for the wicked, right?"

Bennett set Nate down and pulled his son's thick coat and boats off. "Is it Jackson? I see the way you watch him."

Juan swallowed. His pining was becoming

noticeable. He had a feeling too many Wilsons knew how he felt about the younger omega. "Don't worry about it, Bennett. Now, where's this hole in your wall, and how exactly did it get there?"

Bennett gave him a long look. "I see you, Juan Vega." He turned. "It's upstairs. Terry and Hannah were rollerblade sledding with Oggy and Choco, and things got out of control."

"Rollerblade sledding?" Juan asked, chuckling.

"I didn't even know rollerblades were a thing anymore," Bennett said, rolling his eyes. "They put on rollerblades, then harnessed Oggy and Choco. The dogs didn't like it, so they started running. The kids were like *'yay, this is so fun,'* then they crashed into the wall."

"I show," Nate yelled and ran ahead of them. He pointed to a big hole in the wall at the end of the hall. "See?"

"Thanks, Nate," Juan said and patted the kid on the head. "Let's see what we have here."

Bennett watched over his shoulder as he worked. "In all the time you've lived in Hobson Hills, I've only seen you date two people and that was during that first year."

Juan cut around the hole and pulled the loose sheetrock out. "Uh-huh."

"You dated that server in the diner. What was her name?"

"Tracy." That had been fun, but Tracy had been hung up on her ex. When he'd come back into the picture, Juan was booted out.

"Yes, Tracy. She was nice," Bennett said, rubbing his chin. "Then there was the blond that works at the bank."

"Shaina," Juan said, nailing the new piece of sheetrock into place. Shaina and he had gotten along really well until the first nightmare. He'd woken up shaking and crying, and she'd never been back.

Bennett wrinkled his nose. "I don't know why you dated her in the first place."

Juan rolled his shoulders and worked on spreading the mud around the edges of the new piece of sheetrock. "It was something to do."

"That first year, you flirted with a few omegas too," Bennett said, huffing as he sat on the floor. "Hell, you flirted with just about everyone."

"An alpha has needs," he said, mocking his dad.

Bennett snorted. "Ever since you and Jackson started spending time together, you stopped flirting and dating." He pointed at Juan. "You, my darling alpha, have some shit going on in your head."

Juan scowled. Shortly after Jackson moved to Hobson Hills, Juan and he started hanging out. First, it was at their Dolly's Diamonds meetings. Then, it was a movie or dinner or lunch, and before he knew it, Juan didn't *see* anyone but Jackson. He didn't want to hear anyone else laugh at a romantic comedy or talk about coffee addictions over lunch.

"We're just friends, Bennett," Juan said, keeping his words short. He would do anything to keep Jackson in his life, even shut down his own feelings. "Jackson doesn't date alphas."

Plus, Jackson doesn't need my shitty baggage, he thought.

"Hmm," Bennett said, watching him closely. "You know, Nate already made his Christmas wish this year."

Nate danced in place. "Wish for pony."

Juan chuckled. "You asked Santa for a pony, kiddo?"

Nate nodded. "Yeppy. Pony and Nari."

Juan smiled. Nari was the little boy's best friend.

"You can't have Nari, but maybe you'll get a pony," Bennett said, laughing. "Maybe Santa will bring Juan what he wants too if he wishes for it."

Nate gasped. "Yes, yes!" Juan barely caught the little boy before he knocked over the bucket of mud as he jumped into Juan's arms. "Make wish!"

Juan laughed. "Okay. I made a wish, Nate."

The little boy frowned. "Close eyes, be quiet, make wish."

"Better listen to him," Bennett said, grinning. "Don't want to piss off Santa."

Juan chuckled, then closed his eyes. He could see it now. Jackson would be his omega, and the whole world would know it. They would live in the house Jackson rented in town. Juan could fix up the attic to make a kickass master bedroom and bath. Jackson's dog, Miss Mona, and his cat, Onyx, would become Juan's pets too.

A few years from now, they'd have a kid or two. He'd make a nice, sturdy swing set for the backyard and play with the kids every day after work. They'd decorate for the holidays, and Christmas day would be full of the laughter, love, and magic of his own family.

Fuck, please let this happen, he thought, longing shooting through him. *I wish Jackson Potts loved me like I love him. I wish he was mine.*

"Make wish?" Nate asked, patting his cheeks.

Juan opened his eyes. Bennett looked entirely too smug. "Yeah, kiddo. I made my wish."

CHAPTER 2

*J*ackson poured the kibble into the hot pink doggy bowl covered in rhinestones. His Old English sheepdog mix looked at him like he was joking. Her bangs were pulled back into a short ponytail that poked up between her ears.

"Miss Mona, you need to eat the kibble. I'm not buying you a different kind until you eat all of this," Jackson said, giving her a stern look.

"Woof."

"Don't sass me, young lady." He left her to stare at the bowl and got his cat's food ready, placing the heavy stoneware bowl on the counter next to the sink.

Onyx left the sink and sniffed at his food before he began eating.

"See, Miss Mona?" Jackson said, glaring at his dog. "Onyx is a good cat and eats whatever food I buy him."

Miss Mona stared at him until he went to the cabinet and got her wet dogfood. He put half a pouch over her dry food, then put the rest in the refrigerator. "You're supposed to be on a diet, young lady."

She didn't care.

Jackson laughed, then left the kitchen. He admired the healthy plants arranged around the house and ran his fingers across the sage green wall as he headed toward his room. He loved his home. It was all his. He had chosen how to decorate it—from the color of the walls to the new hardwood floors—and in a few more years, he would own it.

Growing up, he had thought he would end up as some abusive alpha's husband, just like his grandpapa and papa. In that life, he would have had no control of anything. He would have been seen as nothing more than a breeding tool.

That's not my life, he thought. *I'm my own man now, and this is my home.*

The house was only a couple of blocks from the bookstore where he worked. It was a small two-story with a huge attic and a nice-sized backyard. There was even a carport at the back of the house leading to one of Hobson Hills's backstreets.

The two bedrooms on the second floor were kind of small, but they were bigger than anything he ever had before, and they had spacious closets at least. The living room had a small stone fireplace and several large windows facing the tiny front yard and the decorated residential street.

Christmas time in Hobson Hills was almost as busy as tourist season. All the locals were shopping and visiting one another. He loved to watch them from behind the curtains. *I'm such a creep.*

He checked the time, then let Miss Mona out in the backyard for her morning poo. He checked on Onyx's litter box and refilled the water dishes.

"You two behave while I'm gone. I'll be back around six." Miss Mona ignored him and hopped onto the couch for an after-breakfast nap. Onyx waved a furry black paw, then went to his favorite sunning spot in the front windowsill.

Jackson smiled happily and locked his door behind him. *Time for breakfast, then on to work.*

He walked a few streets over to Honey Buns and took a minute to sniff the air when he stepped into Zoe's bakery. There was absolutely nothing better in the world than a cinnamon roll and a hot latte. Nothing.

Griff waved from their favorite booth, and Jackson grinned at his friend as he slid in. "Is that latte and muffin mine?"

Griff slid the cup and plate to him. "Of course. I don't drink coffee-flavored milk."

Jackson studied his friend. Griff wore his scrubs and a long-sleeved tee. He looked tired and paler than usual. "What's wrong? Is Bea alright?"

Griff gave him a tight smile. "Bea is okay. She's at Ines's house."

Jackson watched Griff and waited patiently.

Griff groaned and rubbed his face. "I'm pregnant."

Jackson's eyes widened, and he leaned across the

table. "Are you serious? The only guy you've been with since you moved here was… Oh fuck."

Griff sighed. "I know, right? You and Luke are my best friends. I never should have slept with him. We knew we didn't care about each other that way. I just got tired of being alone. It's been a while since my divorce, and I just wanted someone. Damn it, this is bad."

Jackson took Griff's hand, swallowing back the anger building in him. Luke had seemed like a really nice guy, even if he was an alpha. Jackson should have known he was as shitty as the rest of them.

"You and Bea can move in with me. I'll help you take care of the baby." Jackson bit his lip as he mentally rearranged his budget. Having a steady job, no rent, and only himself to take care of had allowed him to put back a nice nest egg. He had planned to use it to buy the house from Gramps, but that would have to wait.

Griff smiled, eyes softening. "You really are a good friend. I'll be alright, Jackson. I have a good job, plenty of support from you and my brothers, and you know Luke will help out."

Jackson snorted. "He's an alpha, Griff. He's going to do what's best for him, and you know his family doesn't even like that he's friends with us. Plus, he wants Britney. He's going to either drop us like we're rotting garbage or ignore the whole situation."

Griff gave him an exasperated look. "You know Luke. You like him. Why would you automatically think he'd do something like that?"

Jackson leaned back in the booth and took a bite of

his muffin. He thought in silence for a few moments. "I didn't think he would, but he got you pregnant."

Griff arched a brow. "It takes two to get pregnant, Jackson. We were friends with benefits and were well aware of the consequences."

Jackson shrugged and finished his muffin, struggling to find the right words. He didn't want to be disappointed by Luke, but it would be hard for the alpha to do right by Griff. "I guess we'll see what happens. Have you told him?"

"Not yet," Griff said, sighing. "I'm two months along and went to the doctor this morning to confirm it. You're the first person I've told. Damn, Zed is going to blow a fuse and try to kill Luke. Then, I'll have to take Bea to visit her uncle in prison. I hope the guards are nice."

Jackson took a breath. "I'm here, Griff. Whatever you need, alright? I have some money saved, and I know Yeo wouldn't mind if I brought Bea or the baby with me to work. You're not alone, okay?"

Griff gave him a grateful smile. "You have no idea how much that means to me, Jackson."

"I'll help Zed hide the body," Jackson added, rubbing his chin. "I bet Gramps has a ton of good spots to bury Luke."

Griff snorted and started laughing. "I can't picture you helping Zed tote Luke's dead body around the woods. You wouldn't want to get your UGGs all dirty."

Jackson sniffed. "I would borrow Papa's stinky cowboy boots."

Griff laughed again. "Damn it, I love you Jackson Potts."

Snickering drew their attention to a few teenagers in the booth behind them. One of the girls whisper yelled, "Did you hear him? I told you they were a couple!"

Jackson exchanged an amused look with Griff. "I'll see you after work, dear."

Griff rolled his eyes and waved Jackson away. "Go count books or whatever. I have to work a twelve-hour shift today."

Jackson pulled him up. "You'll take breaks, right? Remember to eat? Do you want me to bring you dinner after I finish?"

Griff hugged Jackson. "You really are my best friend, Jackson. I'll text you if I need anything, okay? I'm going to be alright. I promise."

Jackson sipped his latte and watched Griff shrug into his thick winter coat and leave the bakery. He didn't like the idea of Griff working so hard while he was growing a person inside him. His papa had busted his ass during each and every one of his pregnancies until the last one. Jackson didn't want that for his friend.

He shook off his thoughts and ordered another latte at the counter.

Zoe watched him as she fixed his drink. "How's my beautiful Jackson today?"

He made a face. "I was a lot better an hour ago. How's it going with you? Has Gib's mom given in to your charms yet?"

Zoe grinned. "I have a plan. She *will* be at Christmas dinner, one way or another."

Jackson took his cup and gave her a wary look. "Tanner will be there too, and you know he's a cop. If you have a kidnapped person tied to a chair at the table, he'll have to call it in."

Zoe shook her head. "That's Plan D. I'll give you a call if that's what it comes to. Your job will be to temporarily blind Tanner."

"How am I supposed to do that?" Jackson asked, laughing.

Zoe shrugged. "That's your job, not mine. You'll have to figure it out."

He groaned and laid his money on the counter. "I'm going to pretend I don't know you."

A few minutes later, he opened the door to the bookstore and flipped the sign to open. This month was one of the busiest times for Jackson's brother's store. Everyone either wanted to find that perfect gift for a loved one or find something to distract them from the stress of the holidays.

As expected, as soon as the doors opened, Jackson was stuck at the register, ringing customers up. A couple of hours later, Amy clocked in, and he took a break to get more coffee and another muffin.

Then, it was back to the bookstore to restock before the first club meeting of the day. This one was meant for younger children, so he set up the kids play area and put out the snacks.

"Amy, go ahead and take a break before the horde descends," he said, walking back behind the counter.

"The Wild Blue Story Time Club officially has twenty-three kids now."

The older woman groaned. "I love kids. I really do."

"Keep that in mind when we flip to see who gets to assist Yeo running it," Jackson said dryly.

Yeo came down the stairs a few minutes later, Linc on his heels. Jackson's older brother looked well-rested and practically glowed with happiness.

"Uncle Jay! Guess what? Guess what?" Linc bounced in place, arms full of the family's pet rabbit, Huckleberry.

Jackson grinned. "What?"

"Artie is going to come with Iggy to story time. He's gonna play us all the sunshine song," Linc said.

Jackson smiled. Artie was a good guy. "The sunshine song? Really?"

"Really! He promised." Linc turned to Yeo. "Papa, can Iggy and I dress up Hucky when he gets here?"

Yeo blinked. "Why does Huckleberry need to dress up?"

"It's cold," Linc said, tone letting them all know that should have been obvious. "Uncle Ernie made him a new sweater."

Jackson shook his head and went back to restocking shelves. Huckleberry probably hated sweaters, but most animals would. Personally, he loved dressing Miss Mona up, but she was special and obviously superior to every other dog in town.

He froze in place, a stack of books in his arms. *What if every pet in town were dressed like bears? Would it be scary or cute? What if Hobson Hills had a pet pageant? Miss*

Mona would obviously win, but would that hurt the other pets' feelings, or would they see it as a growing experience?

"Hey, Jay." Juan's deep voice came from behind him. "Thoughts heavy? You look like that big statue of the guy thinking real hard."

Jackson spun around and tried for a deep, brooding look. "My thoughts are too much for mortal men."

Juan laughed, and warmth settled in Jackson's chest. *Smiling should be illegal*, he thought, wanting to trace Juan's smile with his tongue.

"Is Dolly's Diamonds and Dragons meeting at your house tonight?" Juan asked, still chuckling. "I can never remember the schedule."

Jackson started putting the books on the shelf in front of him. "Yes, it is. Remember to bring the guacamole. Yours is so much better than Rosemary's." He turned back around, eyes wide. "Don't you dare tell her I said that."

Juan grinned. "I'll keep your secret, Jay."

Jackson handed Juan a few of the books. "Make yourself useful and put this out on the top shelf. What are you up to today?"

Juan reached above him, and Jackson paused to breathe in the smell of leather and warm skin. *Why does he have to smell so good?*

"I have to do some work at Ines's house. Thought I'd stop by and say hi to Miss Mona and Onyx."

"You still have your key, right?" Jackson would like to think Juan would have told him if he'd lost it, but who knew?

"Yeah," Juan said, smiling wide. "Can I make the

guac at your place? That way I don't have to carry it around."

"You may." Jackson nodded solemnly. "However, if I eat it all before you get there tonight, that's your own fault."

Juan nodded. "Noted."

LATER THAT NIGHT, Jackson sat in one of his overstuffed chairs and petted Onyx. His black cat leaned into his strokes. The other six members of Dolly's Diamonds and Dragons gathered around the fire and snacked on the food spread out on the coffee table.

Juan sat in front of Jackson's chair with Miss Mona. The alpha's deft fingers separated the long hair falling into her eyes into two topknots. He pinned each one with a purple butterfly hair clip.

Jackson smiled to himself. Juan liked bringing Miss Mona cute clips for her hair.

"I don't know if I can do it," Valentina said, shoulders slumping. The twelve-year-old sat beside her brother-in-law Abel on the couch. "Lona is one of the most popular girls in school. Who has a sleepover on a Sunday?"

"It's winter break," Jackson reminded her. "You don't have school Monday."

Valentina scowled. "I don't know why she even invited me."

"Because you're the prettiest and smartest girl in the world," Abel said, stroking her hair and hugging her.

She gave him an exasperated look. "That's your pregnancy hormones talking."

Jackson grinned. Abel looked as if he was ready to give birth right there on Jackson's new rug.

Abel's eyes watered. "I just love you so much, Valentina."

Drew scooped out the last of the guacamole and sat on Valentina's other side. "Okay, popular middle school girls are the devil. It's a known fact. Not to make you nervous, but are you the only one invited that's *not* in her clique?"

Valentina groaned. "Yeah."

"She's planning some kind of prank," Drew said. "The only question is do you want to deal with it or not."

Valentina shook her head. "Not! I don't want to deal with it at all, but Mateo keeps saying I need more friends, so he's making me go."

Abel sniffed and nuzzled her head. "The best girl in the whole world."

She sighed and pointed at Abel. "This one is completely useless. I don't think I can avoid going."

"Then you deal with it," Drew said, nodding. "You go and keep your eyes open. Try to maneuver around her and make it through until morning."

"It's just a sleepover," Ms. Bird said. The middle-aged woman sat primly in her chair and held the book they were currently reading pressed to her chest. "Surely Lona is just being friendly."

Mrs. Odell cackled. "Hell no, she's not, Rosemary. I've seen that girl around, and she's as self-absorbed and petty as her mother."

"Listen, Valentina," Juan said. "We're called Dolly's Diamonds and Dragons for a reason. She says 'it's hard to be a diamond in a rhinestone world,' and she's right. It's easy to be intimidated by those that are at the top of the pile, but you can't give in. This girl may be popular and have the upper hand, but you're strong and have a beauty all your own."

Valentina blushed and looked at her lap. "I'm nothing special."

Abel growled. "Don't say that."

Jackson knew how she felt. It was hard to be different from everyone else. He had been the kid with the strict, religious alpha dad, and Valentina was the new girl whose parents were murdered. It wasn't going to be easy.

"Think about Alyssa in *Taming the Wild Dragons*," Jackson said. "She didn't hesitate to jump right off that cliff and onto the wild dragon's back, did she?"

Valentina looked up and met his stare. "No, she didn't. I can do this."

Mrs. Odell jumped up. "You bet your ass, you can, Val. Now, come dance with me. I have a hankering to hear 'Hard Candy Christmas.' Put it on, Rosemary."

"Yes, ma'am," Ms. Bird said, laughing. She stood and put the record on.

The room filled with Dolly's voice, and they sang along for a moment before getting up to dance.

Jackson swayed around the room with Onyx, and

he laughed when Juan picked up Miss Mona and tried to do the same with the big dog. Drew and Valentina waltzed around the living room together while Ms. Bird and Mrs. Odell hugged Abel and swayed with him.

These meetings always filled something inside Jackson. He was really good at pretending he was okay, but it was exhausting. These people didn't mind when he was quiet and sad.

A couple of hours later, all the snacks were gone, and Jackson was helping Abel to his car. "Are you sure you're good to drive?"

"You act like I'm drunk," Abel said, growling. "I'm just pregnant, Jackson."

"Uh oh," Valentina said. "The tears and love have gone away, and now it's attitude and crankiness."

Abel grumbled as he got into the car, and Jackson smothered his laughter.

"You need more shelves," Juan said from behind him.

Jackson startled and turned around. "Are you criticizing my book piles?"

Juan's smile made Jackson's toes curl. "Your plants and books keep multiplying, Jay. You have Sunday off? I'll come by and make some more shelves."

"I'll make you dinner," Jackson said, smiling. "You sure you don't mind?"

"Not even a little." Juan pet Miss Mona one more time, then left.

Jackson's dog watched him leave, whining. "I know how you feel, Miss Mona," Jackson whispered. "I know exactly how you feel."

CHAPTER 3

JUAN

"Dean and I are worried about something," Ray said, biting the head off a gingerbread man.

Juan and his friends sat around the kitchen table at Gramps's house, playing poker and eating snacks. Niccolo's large Bernedoodle, Ned, and Gramps's old hound dog, Rufus, lay under the table, waiting to clean up the crumbs.

"What is it?" Niccolo asked, signing for their friend Noah's benefit. Niccolo was the newest addition to their poker nights and fit in well with everyone else. Juan watched him closely. The omega may look all sweet and innocent, but he was a fucking card shark.

"Something's wrong with Jackson," Ray said, sighing.

Juan sat up straight. "Something's wrong? Is he hurt? What is it?"

Ernie elbowed him. "Down boy," he whispered from the side of his mouth.

24

"Dean told me that Yeo told him that Jackson's in love with someone," Ray said, shaking his head.

Ernie's hand barely muffled Juan's growl. The omega leaned over and hugged Juan's head. "I just needed a hug, buddy."

Juan glared through Ernie's arms, tempted to bite the man's bicep. Juan deeply regretted talking to Reuben and Ernie about his feelings for Jackson. *Fuck it*, he thought and bit Ernie.

Ernie yelped and rubbed his arm before sitting back down. He looked at Ray. "So, Jackson's in love with someone?"

Ray nodded, looking disgusted. "Can you believe it? Jackson's so young, and he's just started letting himself be a kid. He doesn't need to be tying himself to anyone right now."

Juan studied his cards. He was very aware that he was over ten years older than Jackson. He needed to remember that when he was alone late at night. He had no business thinking about Ray's stepson, especially if Jackson was in love with someone.

"He's almost twenty-three," Ernie said, rolling his eyes. "Hell, he's more mature than I am. He's taking business classes online and practically manages Yeo's bookstore. He's an adult who can fall in love if he wants to."

"Jackson's a smart young man," Gramps added, reaching for a cookie. "Maybe you ought to trust him."

They finished the round, and Niccolo scooped all the poker chips toward himself.

Carter dealt the next hand. "If Jackson's in love with

someone, why won't he tell Yeo or Dean who it is? It makes me think maybe this person isn't appropriate."

"Exactly," Ray said, voice smug. "This person is taking advantage of Jackson's innocence. I need to hunt them down and kick their ass."

Noah grinned and signed. "Gramps probably knows a good place to hide the body."

"That I do," Gramps said, nodding.

Niccolo groaned. "Your testosterone-fueled idiocy gives me a headache. Jackson can take care of himself, and he won't appreciate you stepping in."

Ray scowled. "I'm his dad. It's my responsibility."

"How old were you when he was born?" Niccolo asked, arching a brow.

Ray sputtered, then folded his hand. "It's the principle of the thing. I don't like saying I'm his step-dad. I'm his dad, damn it."

"Are you boys ready for more cookies?" Grammy asked from the doorway of the kitchen.

"Yes, ma'am," Carter said, grinning. "We should have poker night here every week."

Grammy giggled and put together another tray of snacks. "You boys are fun."

Niccolo helped himself to another cookie. "I told her if she keeps feeding me like this I'll never leave."

"That would be just fine," Grammy said, bending and kissing Niccolo's head. "We love having you and Eliza living here."

Niccolo won another hand and scooped the chips to his pile. "We're going shopping tomorrow, Grammy. Tell Eliza I'm buying her a designer onesie."

THE NEXT MORNING, Juan rinsed his cereal bowl and stuck it in the dishwasher. His apartment was too quiet, and he couldn't stand it. He wasn't supposed to be at Jackson's until two, but he didn't want to wait.

I should have gone to breakfast at Gramps and Grammy's house, he thought. He'd had a rough night last night, so he'd thought a quiet morning would help settle his nerves. *Goes to show I don't know shit.*

He grabbed the bag of hair clips and his keys, then locked the door behind him. He didn't live far from Jackson. When he'd first moved to Hobson Hills, Gramps had helped him find the apartment. The building was owned by Mrs. Odell, and he'd liked living there.

But the place wasn't home anymore. It didn't have Jackson, Onyx, and Miss Mona.

He parked on the street in front of Jackson's home and admired the way the dark blue siding and bright red door contrasted with the white snow. The house was tall and narrow, with a small bay window overlooking the tiny patch of yard in front. It was covered with snow right now, but Juan knew beneath it were well maintained flowerbeds. Jackson liked his plants.

Two bare-limbed maple trees guarded the icy sidewalk, and a white gate at the side of the house led to the backyard. Curtains moved in the window and Miss Mona grinned at him, tongue hanging out.

Juan shut the door to his truck and walked up the

steps, noting that there were still no holiday decorations on the door or windows. Ines's house next door was covered in lights and decorations, as were most of the other houses in the neighborhood.

Jackson met him at the door. "Hey. You're early."

"That okay?"

Jackson snorted. "Of course. Come on in."

Juan looked over his shoulder. "I have to get the shelves out of the truck. I made the mistake of telling Harper you needed more, so he gave me two full bookshelves."

Jackson rolled his eyes. "He's never going to make money if he keeps giving his furniture to his family and friends."

"He does well enough," Juan said. "I love building things, but I don't have his eye for detail. The man has talent."

"Let me put my shoes on, and I'll help you with the shelves," Jackson said.

Together, they carried the two heavy cedar bookshelves into the house. "I thought we'd put them in the living room." Juan looked around. "They match the others in here."

Jackson gave him a playful look. "And you say you don't have an eye for detail."

Miss Mona demanded Juan's attention before he could do anything else. He knelt and hugged her. "Hey, girl. I brought you some pretty hair clips."

"She doesn't deserve new hair clips. She won't eat her diet dogfood." Jackson scowled at the dog, even as he scratched her ears. "Dr. Grover said she needs to lose ten pounds."

Juan cooed at her and rubbed her cheeks. "She's just a floofy girl. What's that mean old vet know anyway?"

Jackson laughed at him. "I'm going to put a pot of chili on the stove. I'll be right back."

"Okay." Juan stood and looked around the room. "Where are all the books you want in the shelves? We'll get everything set up."

"Upstairs, but I'll get them. You can't go in there."

Juan raised his eyebrows. "Oh, really? What are you hiding?"

Jackson gave him a hard look. "Important manly stuff, so don't get any ideas."

As soon as he was alone, Juan and Miss Mona went up the stairs. The two bedrooms and bathroom weren't tiny, but they weren't exactly big either. He'd been up there before when he helped Jackson repaint the place.

"Room on the left," he whispered to Miss Mona. "Let's see what he's hiding. You know anything about this person he's in love with?"

"Woof."

"Hmm, that doesn't sound promising."

Onyx lay in the middle of the bed. The cat blinked at him when he came in and started poking around. He didn't see any signs of anyone being there except Jackson.

"I won't look in the drawer of the nightstand," Juan told Miss Mona. "There are some things I can't know, or I'll drive myself crazy."

He didn't see anything out of place at all. The room

was a little cluttered, but that was Jackson. He opened the closet door. Nothing but clothes and shoes.

"Well, that's a disappointment."

"Woof." Miss Mona wagged her tail and waited for him next to two piles of books. He picked up a stack and went back downstairs.

Jackson met him at the bottom and took the books from him. "I said no snooping."

"How long have you known me?" Juan asked.

"For over two years," Jackson said, shaking his head. "I should know better. You up for a *Walking Dead* marathon after we finish this?"

"Again. How long have you known me?" Juan laughed.

"Let's get these shelves arranged," Jackson said, rolling his eyes.

The two worked together and shuffled furniture around. Jackson was a small guy, but he was sturdy and strong.

Juan moved a heavy pot of ivy to the top of one of the new bookshelves. "I noticed the lack of holiday cheer around here."

"Don't give me shit," Jackson said, making a face. "It seems stupid to put up decorations and everything for just one person. I always go to Papa's house on Christmas morning."

Juan bent to kiss Miss Mona's furry head. "What about Miss Mona and Onyx? Don't they deserve presents and treats?"

Jackson watched him play with Miss Mona's top knots and started laughing. "Juan Vega, the super buff alpha who likes to buy butterfly hairclips for a dog. You are such a sap."

Juan scowled and fluffed Miss Mona's ears. "Don't listen to him, girl. He's just jealous because his hair is too short for hairclips."

"Speaking of hair," Jackson said, eyeing the top of Juan's head. "Why did you get rid of your green? You look different without it."

Juan shrugged. It wasn't at all because he'd overheard Jackson tell Griff he thought James McAvoy was hot. "No reason."

Jackson frowned. "I miss it."

Note to self, dye hair again.

Juan moved a potted fern and tried to think of a good way to get Jackson to talk about this person he was in love with. "You were quiet the other day, like you were upset."

Jackson knelt on the floor and sorted books, face sullen. "Juan, what would you do if you were in love with one person but found out you got another person pregnant?"

Juan fought a wince and rubbed his chest. He knew Jackson was bi, but damn it, he thought the man hadn't been dating anyone. "Uh, that's kind of tough. I would at the very least step up and help with the pregnancy and baby."

Jackson gave him a small smile. "Of course you would. You'd be a good dad, Juan."

"Did you get someone pregnant?" Juan asked, then realized Jackson could be talking about something else entirely. He spun around and scowled. "Are *you* pregnant? Who the hell do I need to kill?"

Jackson laughed. "I'm not talking about me."

Juan blinked. "Oh. That's good."

Jackson leaned his head back. "Don't tell anyone, okay?"

Juan sat next to him on the floor. "Lay it on me, Jay."

"Luke is in love with Britney but got Griff pregnant."

"Whoa," Juan said, wincing. "Griff's brothers aren't going to like that."

Jackson looked away. "I liked Luke. I thought he was a good guy."

"Did you love him?" Juan asked, swallowing hard.

Jackson wrinkled his nose. "No. Why do people keep asking that? I thought Luke was one of my best friends, but then he goes and does something like this. I can't stand it, Juan."

Juan frowned. "Has he said he won't help Griff?"

Jackson shrugged. "Not yet, but it's going to happen. You don't know his parents, but I do, and they're snobs. They don't like that he hangs out so much with Griff and me. This will piss them off."

Juan wrapped an arm around Jackson's shoulders. "I don't know the man, but maybe we should give him a chance. Maybe he'll surprise you."

Jackson picked up Onyx and settled the cat in his lap before leaning his head on Juan's shoulder. "Why can't all alphas be like you?"

Juan winced up at the ceiling. *Why can't all omegas be like you?*

"You know what's even worse?" Jackson said quietly.

"What?"

"When Griff told me he was pregnant, I was mad and worried for him, but after I thought about it…"

Juan frowned, waiting for Jackson to finish his thought.

"I was jealous," Jackson whispered, turning his face into Juan's shoulder. "Griff already has Bea. I want my own baby. Isn't that stupid? I don't want an alpha, but I want a damn baby."

Juan leaned his head against Jackson's. "That's not stupid. I'll tell you a secret. I'm fucking jealous of Carter and Elijah. They already have Olive and the twins, but Elijah's pregnant again."

Jackson looked up, his green eyes so dark they were almost black. "You want kids?"

"Hell yeah," Juan said. "I've always wanted a bunch. My dad always told me that was an alpha's main purpose." *Making babies and running the household.*

"There's more to you than that," Jackson said, licking his lips.

Juan lost his train of thought, eyes tracing Jackson's tongue.

"You're more than a stud horse," Jackson said and leaned up, pressing his lips to Juan's.

Juan froze, unable to think about anything but the taste of Jackson's sweet mouth. A warm tongue slid into his mouth, and he groaned, sinking into Jackson's kiss.

Jackson moved to straddle Juan's lap and a loud

yowl startled them both. Onyx gave them a grumpy look and stalked away.

Jackson's face turned red. "Um, I'll go check on dinner."

Juan ran a hand through his hair. "Yeah. Okay. I'll, uh, finish with the books here, then go get that other pile."

A couple of hours later, Juan left Jackson's house.

That was the most awkward dinner and the shortest Walking Dead marathon I've ever had, he thought.

Jackson hadn't said a thing about the kiss. He'd barely talked at all, and he'd been as stiff as a board for the rest of the afternoon. *Not the good kind of stiff either.*

Juan let himself into his apartment and fell face-first onto the coach. "Fuck my life."

CHAPTER 4

After Juan left, Jackson collapsed onto his couch. "Onyx, what the hell is wrong with me?"

His cat glared at him from the windowsill.

"Are you still mad I squashed you? His lips were right there. I couldn't help it."

Miss Mona jumped up to sit beside him and licked his cheek.

"Thank you, girl. At least you understand." He rubbed his face. "What was I thinking?"

I was thinking he was so close and smelled so good. A knock at the door interrupted his thoughts.

He opened the door and threw himself into his grandfather's arms. "Grandpapa. I'm an idiot."

Min-Jun hugged him tightly. "Jackson, what's wrong?"

Jackson pulled Min-Jun inside. "Were you visiting your *girlfriend*?" He couldn't help but tease.

Min-Jun blushed. "Ines and I had an early dinner,

yes, but don't try to distract me. What's wrong, sweetheart?"

They sat on the couch, and Miss Mona laid her head on his lap. "I don't want an alpha."

Min-Jun nodded, his thin face solemn. "Alright. I can understand why you wouldn't. Your alpha father and grandfather were horrible people."

"They were." Jackson played with Miss Mona's ears. "They hurt you and Papa, and they were both so controlling. Everything had to be exactly the way they wanted it. It was like the whole world revolved around them."

"To them, it did," Min-Jun said simply. "You don't have to be with an alpha, Jackson. You can be with whoever you want."

Jackson wiped at his eyes. "I'm in love with a damn alpha. I'm also his friend, and I don't want to lose that. I *need* to have him in my life."

"Oh, dear. I see now." Min-Jun sighed and took his hand. "Have you talked with your Papa about this?"

Jackson shook his head. "I don't want to. He feels so guilty that he stayed with *him* for so long. I don't want Papa to know I'm fucked up."

"Watch your language," Min-Jun said sternly, then leaned over and kissed his cheek. "First, you aren't *fucked up.*"

Jackson snickered when Min-Jun's nose scrunched up as he cursed. His grandfather was one of the most polite and proper people he knew.

Min-Jun gave him a look, then continued. "I can't imagine anyone would be surprised that you have trouble trusting alphas. Dean probably knows it already, Jackson."

He shrugged. "I don't want him to worry about it."

Min-Jun sighed. "Worrying is what parents do, baby. Trust me."

"He's so happy with Ray," Jackson said wistfully, thinking of his papa and stepdad. "That's what made me believe that maybe I could find someone of my own. They fit together."

"They do," Min-Jun said with a smile. "Remember, though, it was hard for Dean to trust another person, not only with his heart and body, but with you boys. I think he would understand exactly how you're feeling."

"What about you, Grandpapa? You were with the other asshole for most of your life." Jackson loved Ines, but he never would have pictured her with Min-Jun.

Min-Jun smiled, dark eyes sparkling. "Ines is *my* choice."

Jackson grinned. He loved it when the feistiness seeped through Min-Jun's prim and proper mask.

"My parents sent me to your grandfather when I was barely legal," Min-Jun said. "I had never met him and would never have chosen him myself. It took a long time to realize that I was strong enough and smart enough to be my own person. I still struggle with it, but Dean and you boys make it easier." Min-Jun was quiet for a moment. "Ines and I started as friends. She helped me come out of my shell and discover who I was. I learned what kinds of things I like to do and what my own preferences were. I was able to remember the young man I was before I was sent to your grandfather."

Jackson bit his lip. Juan had been right there beside Jackson from the moment they had arrived in Hobson Hills. He'd helped him move into the house and fix it up. He spent countless nights with Jackson watching television or playing videogames, and he was always Jackson's test subject when he was experimenting with cooking. Juan had been his confidant long before Jackson had formed Dolly's Diamonds and Dragons.

"One morning," Min-Jun said, "Ines and I met for coffee, and she was telling me a story about Rue and Auggie. She was laughing, and, I don't know, the light hit her just right, and suddenly I noticed that she was the most beautiful person I had ever seen."

Jackson's eyes watered. "Really?"

Min-Jun looked happy, really and truly happy. "I just sat there, dumbstruck. How had I never noticed the way her eyes danced or how her lips curved when she smiled?"

Jackson laughed. "It was his smile that got me. He has this stupid smirk. He said something to Ray about his cheesy jokes, then smirked. Damn, I thought I'd melt right there."

Min-Jun chuckled. "I know what you mean."

"How did you go from friends to more?" Jackson asked. All he knew was one day Min-Jun announced he had a date and would be home later than usual.

Min-Jun groaned. "I made a fool of myself. A man at the grocery store flirted with her, and I yelled at him. I've never been so embarrassed in my life."

Jackson gasped. "Please tell me someone recorded it? You almost got in a fight, Grandpapa. Was the guy big? Do you think you could have taken him?"

Min-Jun shoved him. "Hush, you."

Jackson laughed. "That did the job though, didn't it? Ines knew you had the hots for her."

Min-Jun blushed. "Yes. Fortunately, she gave me a chance, and we've been dating ever since."

Jackson leaned against Min-Jun's shoulder. "I kissed him – my alpha. It was out of nowhere, and I think it creeped him out."

"Hmm." Min-Jun stroked his hair. "There's no how-to manual for this kind of thing, baby boy. Maybe you should talk to this alpha and figure out if there's something there or not."

If Juan didn't want him, even a little, Jackson would deal with it. He could laugh off the kiss, and they'd go back to being friends. "What if there is something there?" he asked quietly.

"That's scary, isn't it?"

Jackson nodded. "Yeah. The way I feel about him frightens me. I should know better than to blindly trust any alpha, but I can't seem to stop loving him."

"Talk to him, then take your time. There's no reason you have to jump straight into a relationship," Min-Jun said.

A knock at the door made both men jump.

Jackson gave a half-hearted laugh. "It's not usually so busy here."

Luke's face appeared in the window. "I know you're in there, Jackson. Let me in!"

Jackson groaned. He had been dodging Luke's calls and texts for the last few days.

"Please tell me Luke isn't your alpha," Min-Jun said, wincing. "He's a nice man, but he's in love with that nice park ranger."

"Luke is definitely *not* my alpha," Jackson said, snorting. "I better let him in. He's stomping all over my flowerbeds."

Jackson opened the door, and Luke pushed through. "Why haven't you answered the phone? I have an emergency situation, man." He saw Min-Jun. "Oh, I'm sorry. Hi, Mr. Wagner."

Min-Jun stood and smiled. "I was just leaving, Luke. I'll see you tomorrow morning at the bookstore, Jackson. Call me if you need me."

Jackson hugged Min-Jun. "I love you, Grandpapa." He shut the door behind him and turned to Luke. "What do you want?"

Luke frowned. "Are you mad at me?"

Jackson shrugged. "What does it matter?"

Luke gave him a hurt look. "You and Griff are my best friends. Of course it matters."

Jackson rubbed his eyes, suddenly feeling like a shithead. "Did you talk to Griff?"

"Yeah," Luke said, picking up Onyx before sitting. "I'm gonna be a dad, Jackson. How awesome is that?"

Jackson narrowed his eyes. "Awesome?"

Luke grinned. "Griff wants to keep the baby. We're gonna be dads."

"What does Britney think about that?" Jackson

asked, giving him a disbelieving look. "I thought you loved her."

Luke tilted his head, looking confused. "I do love her. Why would me being a dad mean I don't love her?"

Jackson threw his hands in the air, exasperated. "You can't be with Griff *and* Britney."

Luke laughed. "Doc Grover and his ladies are a throuple, so don't tell me I *can't* be with both of them. I know what you mean though. Griff and Britney don't care about one another that way, and Griff and I are just friends."

Jackson glared at his friend. "I'm going to strangle you if you don't explain why the hell you're happy about this."

Luke smirked. "Okay, okay. I thought it was obvious, but clearly, it's not. Griff and I are going to co-parent the baby. We both have good jobs, and we'll share custody. I'm worried Bea will feel left out though. Do you think Griff would mind if she stayed with me and the baby sometimes too? You know his ex is a jackass, and she needs to know she's loved."

Jackson leaned back and squeezed his eyes shut to keep the tears in. "Luke, you're… a really good guy. I'm sorry I thought you were a useless alphahole."

Luke punched his arm. "You thought I'd abandon Griff and the baby? Really?"

Jackson opened his eyes, hating that he had hurt his friend. "I'm sorry."

Luke leaned his shoulder against Jackson's. "Question. If it had been Juan in my position, what would you have thought?"

Jackson closed his eyes again and smiled. "First, I'd be pissed he got Griff pregnant. Griff knows I'm crazy in love with Juan."

"That *would* be a problem," Luke agreed.

"Otherwise, I don't want to think about it," Jackson said quietly. "He wants kids, but he's not the one in this situation anyway. It's you."

Luke sighed. "Why did you think I'd be a douche nozzle?"

Jackson looked at him. "I never told you about the alphas in my family, did I?"

"No," Luke said, making a face. "You told Griff, but not me."

"My biological grandfather bought my Grandpapa from his parents in Korea. He treated him like shit, and Grandpapa thought he had no choice but to stay and be an obedient omega. Then Grandfather made my papa marry a horrible man even though Papa didn't want to."

"Now, that's a douche nozzle."

"I know." Jackson sighed. "It gets more involved. Papa was raped and got pregnant with Yeo."

Luke's face turned red. "The man's dead, right? Please tell me he's dead so I don't gotta murder him."

Jackson nodded. "He's dead. He was Yeo's dad. When Papa got pregnant, Grandfather made him give the baby up. He had convinced Papa that an omega couldn't raise a baby alone. Once that was done, he forced Papa to marry *him*."

"Your biological father?" Luke asked.

"Yeah." Jackson was quiet for a moment. "He hurt

Papa all the time. He was abusive, Luke – emotionally, verbally, and physically."

"Fuck."

"Papa tried to hide it from us kids, but I saw it all. I protected Jimmy, Jake, and Jules as much as I could, but I saw it all."

"He's dead too," Luke said, wrapping his arms around Jackson. "You told me he was."

"When he died, it should have made things easier, but he had gone out of his way to make it almost impossible for us to survive without him," Jackson said. "People in town didn't want to hire us and my fucking grandfather was still there and wanted to step right back into controlling Papa."

"That's when Yeo and the Wilsons went and got you guys," Luke said, understanding. "You came here and now you're all free from that shit."

"It's hard to believe all alphas aren't like them." He hugged Luke. "I'm sorry I didn't trust you."

Luke shrugged. "You had reasons. Thanks for telling me, Jackson. You didn't have to, but I'm glad you did."

Jackson nudged him with his shoulder. "What did your parents say?"

Luke winced. "I haven't told them."

"You know they don't like Griff and me."

"They just don't know you guys well enough," Luke said, biting his lip. "It's their grandbaby though. They love my sister's kids and keep bugging my older brother and his omega to have a bunch."

"What will you do if they get mad at you?" Jackson asked.

Luke stroked Onyx's head. "I'm a grown man. They can deal with it. Let's talk about you and Juan. Ms. Ines told me she saw him leaving your house a few days ago."

"When did you talk to Ines?"

"You didn't answer my texts, Jackson. I had to check to make sure you weren't dead in the bathtub or something. Miss Mona kept telling me she was starving when I looked through the window."

"She always looks hungry," Jackson said. "Begging is the one trick I taught her."

Luke bent to pet Miss Mona where she sat next to the couch. "You're a very talented girl, aren't you?"

"Want to watch *The Walking Dead*?" Jackson asked.

"Sure," Luke said and jumped up, Onyx still in his arms. "I'm making popcorn."

A few hours later, Jackson's phone rang, and he groaned. "Why can't I just wallow in zombies for one night?"

Luke sniffed from where he was curled up with Miss Mona and Onyx on the couch. "I bet you'll answer that call."

Jackson frowned at the number and answered. "Valentina? Are you okay?"

"I need help," Valentina said. Jackson could hear the tears in her voice. "It's a Dolly's Diamonds and Dragons emergency."

CHAPTER 5

JUAN

Juan glared and kicked the board in front of him. "This wood sucks. Can't we get some from Harper?"

He stood with Carter in the cold parking lot of Farm Fresh. The Wilsons' store was closed, but the Christmas tree farm next to it was busy. The stack of lumber they'd had delivered there had turned out to be the cheapest the store had. Now, most of it was warped.

Carter glared at him. "It's Sunday night. If we were working on these later in the week, as planned, maybe I'd feel okay about calling Harper and begging him for some cedar."

"These booths need to be ready by next weekend." Juan shrugged and texted Harper. "I'm asking Harper for wood."

"On a Sunday night? Don't you think he may have plans?" Carter groaned and picked the warped board up. "I had plans for tonight. I was going to pamper my omega and watch holiday movies with the kids. The booths for the Winter Festival were on the to-do list for Tuesday. What crawled up your ass and died?"

Juan put his phone up. "Harper said he has plenty of cedar that he's willing to share for a good cause. He said we can put them together in his *heated* workshop. He even offered to help. That's what a good friend does, Carter."

"Come on," Carter said, sighing. "I'll drive. You can tell me what the hell is wrong with you."

Juan got into Carter's work van and buckled up. "Nothing's wrong with me. We just have a lot of work to do, and I don't want to get behind."

Carter pulled onto the road. "Juan. I love you, man, but you are *not* good at being upset about something. You don't want to talk about it, but you still focus on it and drive the people around you crazy. Just pretend you're Ray for a minute and tell me what the hell is wrong with you."

"Dad says a real man doesn't yammer on about shit," Juan said, watching the dark woods as they drove. "An alpha is supposed to be strong for his omega."

Carter frowned. "You never talk about your dad. No offense, but he sounds stupid."

Juan looked at his friend. "How is that not offensive?"

"I'm just saying." Carter shrugged.

"You ever think about that last mission?" Juan asked, then mentally cursed himself. He didn't need to go there. He didn't need to bring up that shit.

Carter was quiet for a moment. "Yeah. Sometimes I dream about it."

"Me too," Juan said, voice hoarse. "I keep seeing Dylan and Julio."

"That was rough," Carter said, hands gripping the steering wheel. "You were with them when they…"

"Yeah." Juan licked his dry lips. "It was messy."

"Usually when I have one of the nightmares, Elijah wakes me up, and we talk about our plans for the week," Carter said. "It helps remind me where I am."

"I don't have an Elijah," Juan said, staring back out the window.

"No, but you have me. You have Ray. You can call us any damn time you want," Carter said. "I may bitch and moan, but I'm here for you. I've been exactly where you are."

"More yammering," Juan said, giving a shaky laugh. "My dad would tell us to suck it up and be alphas."

"Yeah," Carter said. "Your dad is stupid. It's a fact now." They pulled into Harper's driveway. "Is that why we're here working on these damn booths?"

"No," Juan said, then got out, leaving Carter stuttering. He wasn't about to tell Carter he was scared to death Jackson would never speak to him again. He couldn't seem to focus, and he didn't want to be alone.

Harper met them at the door to his workshop. "Hey, guys. I got to thinking after you called. Usually, we just put the booths together quickly, but then they're falling apart by the time next year rolls around. What if we take some time and do it right? I have some ideas."

Carter sighed. "I'm not going to get to snuggle with Elijah tonight, am I?"

Juan smacked his shoulder. "Nope."

A few hours later, a few more Wilsons had arrived to help and they had six of the booths designed and roughly put together. Each one would need more detailed work, but they were getting there.

"Do we really need twenty booths for the festival?" Carter asked, taking the piece of cedar Harper had just finished cutting.

"The better question is, do we really need to decorate each one?" Gramps said, arching his back and groaning. "You kids have too much damn energy."

"It's going to look good," Juan said, grinning.

He could just see everything set up now. He'd buy Jackson a latte and a cinnamon roll from Zoe's gorgeous booth and explain how he helped Harper carve the holly along the side. Jackson would tell him he was the most talented alpha in the world. Then, Juan would take him on a cozy sleigh ride and they'd curl up together. Maybe Miss Mona would be there too. Ray and Dean could ride by on their horses and nod at Juan in approval. Well, Ray would be riding his donkey, but still.

Jay will love it, he thought, then shook himself. He'd be lucky if Jackson ever spoke to him again.

His phone buzzed, and he looked at the number. "Fuck." His fingers fumbled as he answered it. "Hey, Jackson." Did his voice really sound that uncertain and teenager-like?

"Juan, I need your help. Valentina has a problem,

and I can't fix it alone." Juan didn't like the worry he heard in Jackson's voice.

"Sure, I'm on my way. Where are you?" He looked up and froze. Carter and the others watched him closely. Gramps was struggling not to grin. Uh oh.

"I'm at that little bitch Lona's house. I'll text you the address. You'll have to climb up the tree in the back yard. I'll let you in the window of the upstairs bathroom."

Juan blinked. "Wait. You'll let me in the window? What the hell is going on?"

"I'll tell you when you get here. Bring your tools." Jackson hung up, and Juan stared at his phone.

Carter cleared his voice. "So, you and Jackson, huh? Do you know what your face looked like when you answered? It was like Hotdog's face when we give him a pig ear."

Juan flushed and put his phone in his back pocket. "I'm taking your van. I don't know when I'll be back."

Harper wolf whistled. "Go get him, big guy."

Juan ignored their laughter and grabbed Carter's keys from his hand. A quick drive later, Juan parked on the side of the road. All the lights were on in the big house, and he could hear music thumping from where he sat.

"Parents have to be pissed," he mumbled and grabbed his toolbox. He had no idea what would be needed, so he took everything he could fit in it.

He snuck around to the backyard and looked up. Jackson's face was pressed to the window closest to a large, bare oak tree.

Jackson opened the window. "Climb the tree, Juan," he whisper yelled.

Juan set his toolbox down and went back to the van to get the ladder from the top. *My ass isn't climbing a damn tree. I'm thirty-four, damn it,* he thought.

He set the ladder down and ignored Jackson's glare as he hauled himself and the toolbox up the ladder.

"You could have just climbed the tree," Jackson said, pouting.

"You climbed it, didn't you?" Juan asked.

"He fell six times," Valentina said from where she stood in the bathtub. She was dressed in a pair of black pajamas and had clearly been crying.

Juan climbed through the window and looked around the bathroom. "What the hell happened?"

The small bathroom had about an inch of water on the floor, and the toilet was shooting out more. Soggy tampons were scattered around.

"Lona told me to use this bathroom," Valentina said, almost wailing. "I should have known better. All the other girls were using the downstairs bathroom. I peed, then flushed and this happened. I tried to scoop the water up, but there isn't a bucket or anything. There was a box of tampons in the cabinet, so I dumped them on the floor so they'd absorb the water, but that didn't work."

"She called me, but I don't know how to fix this," Jackson said, trying to use the tampon box to scoop water into the sink.

Valentina started crying again. "She's checked on

me three times now. She's gonna tell everyone I broke her bathroom, and they'll think I'm disgusting."

Someone knocked on the door, and Juan glared at it.

"Valentina, are you coming out tonight?" Lona asked. Juan could hear the laughter in her voice. "Is there a problem?"

"I'm going to take a shower," Valentina said, squeezing her eyes closed. "I'll be down soon."

They listened to the girl's footsteps fade.

Juan took a breath. "We got this, Valentina. You stand right there and hold my toolbox."

He picked Jackson up and he yelped. "What are you doing?"

"You stay out of the way." Juan put him in the bathtub with Valentina. "Let me show you my mad plumbing skills. I'm not Carter, but I know a few things."

It took Juan twenty minutes to find the problem and fix it and another fifteen minutes to hurriedly clean up the water from the floor with towels they found under the sink.

"Okay. Valentina, go ahead and shower, then get back out there," Jackson said, hugging the girl. "The crisis has been averted. Call me if you need me."

"Thank you, guys. Don't tell Mateo or Abel, okay? I don't want them to go berserk on Lona's parents if she really didn't mean to set this up."

"We promise," Juan said before Jackson could protest. "We'll let you deal with it your way, won't we, Jay?"

Jackson scowled. "I guess."

Juan helped Jackson out the window and held the ladder steady while he climbed down to the snow-covered yard. Then, he made his own way down to the ground.

Juan handed Jackson his toolbox and grabbed the ladder. They crouched low as they passed the living room windows.

Voices carried over the music. "Lona, why did you send your friend to the upstairs bathroom? You know the toilet in that one is messed up."

"Mom, don't worry about it," Lona said, voice bored. "It's just a prank. I'll clean it up tomorrow."

"That doesn't sound very nice," Lona's mother said.

"We're just joking," Lona said, groaning. "Can we order more pizza?"

Jackson glared at him.

"Come on, tiger," Juan whispered. "Valentina has this covered."

The reached Carter's van, and Juan put the ladder back on top of it and the toolbox in the back.

Jackson tugged on his sleeve. "We need to talk."

Juan didn't know if he should be relieved or worried. "We smell like toilet water, but the pub stays open for a few more hours."

"Meet you there in an hour," Jackson said and turned.

Juan breathed out heavily and got in the car, driving quickly to his apartment. *Fuck, I hope Christmas wishes are an actual thing.*

CHAPTER 6

JACKSON

*J*ackson sat at the table closest to the door and ordered two coffees. He tugged on the sleeves of his flannel shirt. *What the fuck am I doing?*

He knew two things for certain. He loved Juan, and he was afraid to give control to an alpha, even one he trusted. What he didn't know was how Juan felt about him. He'd returned Jackson's kiss, but he could have just been horny. Who the fuck knew?

North set a large cup of coffee in front of him. "You come to a pub on a Sunday night to drink coffee?"

Jackson shrugged, trying to look nonchalant.

The alpha gave him a skeptical look.

"Don't judge me, North," Jackson finally said. "I'll tell Griff you're being mean to me."

North winced. "Please don't. He already yelled at me for making a joke about Laura being short."

"Why are you always putting your foot in your mouth when Griff stops by?" Jackson asked, laughing.

North groaned. "Extreme bad luck. Fortunately, my boss knows I'm not an asshole or I'd have been fired by now."

Juan walked in, and Jackson forgot North was standing there. Damn, but Juan always looked good. Jackson did miss his green hair, but those damn shoulders and the leather coat always made him shiver.

"I'll just get out of your way," North said, amused.

Jackson waved him away. "I ordered you some coffee."

Juan smiled and sat. "Thanks."

"So," Jackson said, drawing the word out.

"So." Juan nodded, agreeing.

They silently sipped their coffee for a long moment.

"I'm really sorry if I made you feel uncomfortable, Juan," Jackson finally said. "I shouldn't have just kissed you like that."

Juan shrugged. "We're two healthy men, and we were sitting close together."

Jackson nodded furiously. "Yes. Exactly. We have needs, and it's been a really long time since I've kissed someone."

"Me too," Juan said, swallowing hard before he took another drink of his coffee. "There's no reason for this to be awkward."

"You're right," Jackson said. "I mean, Griff and Luke are friends still, and they even fucked around. It's not a big deal at all. Just a kiss."

"Yeah," Juan said, staring at the table.

Jackson's eyes watered, but he forced his tears away. *It was so much more than a kiss.*

"Hey, Juan." One of the servers stopped at their table with a plate. She was a bubbly redhead with a nice smile. "Do you want these cheese sticks? I messed up an order, so these are extras."

Jackson's eyes narrowed on the woman, who only looked friendly and nice. Obviously, she was evil and should be locked in the bathroom until Juan left.

Juan smiled. "Thanks, Connie. I'll pay for them. I'm kind of hungry anyway. I appreciate it."

She blushed and bit her lip, eyes going hot. "No, don't worry about it. I get off in another hour if you wanted to hang out."

Juan shook his head. "Thanks, but I can't. I have an early morning tomorrow."

She looked disappointed. "Oh, okay. I'll see you around."

Jackson glared at her as she left, then grabbed one of the cheese sticks.

"It really has been a while," Juan said, continuing their conversation. "It's hard meeting people in a small town."

Jackson looked over his shoulder at Connie, then back to Juan. "Yeah, sure." *You're an idiot, but I still love you, Juan.*

"You haven't dated much," Juan said, grabbing a cheese stick. "If you… If you get lonely or something, we could help each other out." He looked panicked for a moment. "Not that you couldn't find someone. You're a great guy, and any man or woman would be stupid not to want you. I just mean, it gets hard sometimes, to be alone."

Jackson sat frozen, mind swirling with ideas. They could *help* each other on the couch while watching television or in the kitchen after dinner. They could *help* each other all night long, and Juan could just stay the night and sleep with Jackson. As long as he kept Juan out of the guestroom closet, Juan could stay over every single night so they could *help* each other.

"Yeah, okay," he said before thinking. "I'm lonely. Right now. Help me, please."

Juan blinked, then looked around. "Seriously? Wait, here?"

"My place," Jackson said, jumping up and throwing some cash on the table. He grabbed three more of the cheese sticks and shoved them in his mouth. He'd need energy.

Jackson watched him, clearly struggling not to laugh.

"Meet me there," Jackson said around the food in his mouth and ran for the door. He thought it was supposed to snow overnight, and with luck, Juan would be snowed in at Jackson's house for days. He would have to share his clothes and razor, but he had an extra toothbrush in the half bathroom downstairs.

He jumped into his car and waited until a dazed Juan left the pub before starting the short drive home. He parked in the carport, leaving space for the van, then ran inside.

"Miss Mona! Onyx! Juan's coming to stay the night." Jackson stared hard at his two pets. Onyx was currently licking his ass on the windowsill, and Miss

Mona watched him from the couch where she lay on her back, feet in the air.

"You two need to be on your best behavior so we don't scare him off." Jackson started for the stairs. "Daddy really needs this, okay?"

He ran into the guestroom and made sure the closet door was shut and locked, then ran into his bedroom to dig around for lube and condoms.

"Jay?" Juan's voice carried up the stairs.

Jackson swore under his breath, then quickly shucked his flannel shirt and long-sleeved shirt. "Coming."

He unlaced his UGGs and slipped out of them, then wiggled out of his jeans, leaving him in his socks and Edgar Allan Poe boxer briefs.

He grabbed the lube and condoms, then ran downstairs. "Hey," he said, sliding to a stop in front of Juan. "I have condoms and lube."

Juan watched him, eyes wide. "Jay, what's happening here?"

Jackson frowned. "You're going to help me get over my loneliness with a little frotting, a BJ, and maybe some anal?"

Juan swallowed, then nodded. "Okay. Yeah. Let's do that."

Jackson was on him in seconds, wrapping his arms and legs around Juan and pushing his tongue into his mouth. *Fuck, he tastes so good.*

Juan's hands cupped Jackson's ass, and he held him up, their dicks pressed together. "Are you sure?" he asked between kisses.

Jackson snorted. "Absolutely." He threaded his fingers through Juan's short hair and pulled his head down for another kiss.

Juan's hands squeezed Jackson's ass, and somehow, they managed to make it to one of the chairs in the living room. He fell back into the chair, and Jackson moved his legs quickly so he was straddling Juan.

Jackson moved his lips to Juan's neck and bit down as he began moving his hips, rubbing his hard dick against Juan. He groaned when fingers traced down his spine and slipped into the back of his boxers.

Jackson wanted everything at once. He wanted to know how Juan's dick tasted, wanted to feel his alpha inside him.

"Slow down a bit, Jay," Juan said, voice deep and rumbling. "We have time."

Jackson leaned back and helped Juan out of his jacket and shirt, then traced his mouth over the dark and jagged tattoos covering one side of Juan's chest. His hands smoothed across Juan's broad shoulders, and he nibbled on one of his alpha's hardened nipples.

Juan cupped his head and pulled him up for another wet kiss. "I've dreamed of this for a long time, Jay."

"Really?" Jackson bit his chin. "Me too."

He slid down and wedged himself between Juan's legs. He could see the shape of Juan's dick through his jeans and leaned forward, pressing his mouth along the thick length.

"Fuck, Jay," Juan said and pulled him up on his lap again. "Too much of that, and we won't get far."

He slid his briefs down, baring his dick, and Juan

unbuttoned his jeans. Jackson stroked Juan's dick, then pressed it against his own, jacking them together.

He was getting so close. Juan stopped him and slid a lubed finger into Jackson's ass. *Oh, damn. I need him so much.* A little while later, he got his wish. Juan slid slowly inside him, hands holding tight to Jackson's ass.

It took a moment to adjust, then Jackson started moving, slowly riding his alpha. He kept his lips on Juan's and enjoyed every fucking inch of his alpha's dick. *I love him, I love him, I love him.* This was Juan, not some stranger or a mediocre toy. This was his alpha.

They moved together perfectly, bodies matching each other's movements for seconds or hours, Jackson couldn't tell. Juan bit down on Jackson's bare shoulder when he came, and Jackson splattered against their stomachs.

They sat for a while, pressed together, cum and sweat quickly drying. Jackson didn't want to move. If he moved, then it would end, and it may never happen again.

"I get lonely a lot," he whispered.

Juan gave a shaky laugh. "Me too, but that's okay, isn't it? We have each other now."

"Yes," Jackson hissed, smiling against his alpha's neck. "We have each other."

A little while later, Juan cleared his throat. "We should probably shower, right?"

"Yes, then go straight to bed," Jackson said. "It's probably snowed ten feet, so you'll need to stay here tonight. Maybe even the rest of the week."

Juan snorted. "It's not snowing. I'm looking out the window right now."

Jackson stroked Juan's face and covered his eyes. "Shh. I have plenty of food and wood for the fire. We can sleep naked to conserve our warmth. We'll survive."

CHAPTER 7

JUAN

A few days later, Juan slowly woke up and reached for Jackson. He cracked an eye open when he saw the bed was empty, then grumbled and rolled to his back.

He heard heavy panting and felt warm breath tickling his face. He kept his eyes closed but couldn't help but smile. "Miss Mona, your breath kinda stinks."

A dramatic gasp from the doorway of the bedroom drew his attention. Jackson already had his pajama bottoms on and stood with Onyx in his arms. "Miss Mona says you need to apologize."

Juan turned to the dog panting in his face. Today, her bangs were held back with a headband with a unicorn horn. "I'm sorry. Your breath is like a fresh meadow breeze."

"That's better," Jackson said. "Do you want to meet Griff at the diner for breakfast before you have to go to work? What are you doing today anyway? It's too cold outside to plumb things."

Juan sat up and started scratching Miss Mona's ears. "Your knowledge of plumbing impresses me, blue jay."

Jackson rolled his eyes. "Breakfast?"

Juan yawned. "Yeah. I'll get dressed."

"I did laundry yesterday, so you have some clean clothes folded in the middle two drawers in the dresser." Jackson spun around. "I'll feed the kids."

Miss Mona woofed at the word *feed* and quickly followed Jackson.

Juan buried his face back in his pillow before sliding out of bed. After their first night together, Jackson had made it clear he was lonely every night and needed Juan's *help*, so Juan hadn't been back to his apartment for more than a few minutes.

Not that he minded. Juan had no idea what he was thinking when he'd propositioned Jackson that night. He wanted so much more than a fuck buddy.

Jackson's house felt more like a home than the apartment, but it *was* missing a few things. Since the Wilsons had jumped in to help with the Winter Festival booths, Jackson had a few hours free this afternoon.

Ines had cornered him yesterday when he let Miss Mona out for a poop and told him that something had to be done. Every other house on the street was lit up and decorated except Jackson's.

Juan and Ines now had a plan.

He quickly showered and dressed, taking the time to look for his red sweater. Jackson said he liked it, so Juan had starting wearing it more often. He dug through the drawers.

"Not here." He quickly looked through the closet but didn't see it there either. He closed his eyes. "If I were a sweater, where would I be? I'd be in a closet." He went to the guest room and tried to open the closet. He frowned when he found it locked. He went back to the door and called down the stairs. "Blue jay, why's your closet door locked?"

A crash sounded, and Juan heard heavy steps running up the stairs. Jackson tripped over the top step and face planted before scrambling back up. "Don't look in there."

Juan raised a brow. "Now I *have* to look in there."

"No, no, no," Jackson said. "Come on, let's go have sex. Anywhere you want."

Juan grinned. "Tempting, blue jay, but I wanna know what you're hiding."

Jackson whined for a minute. "I think I saw Bigfoot outside."

Juan frowned. "Nice try, but there's no way Bigfoot is this close to town."

"Juan, you really don't want to look in there," Jackson said, shoulders slumping. "It's embarrassing."

Juan lifted Jackson's face and kissed him. "You can show me what's in there when you're ready, okay? I'm curious as hell, but I'm not gonna push you."

Jackson held up Juan's red sweater. "Wear this and let's go get breakfast."

Juan kissed him again, then followed him to the bedroom to finish getting dressed.

"You should bring some more clothes over," Jackson

said, buttoning his flannel shirt. "That way we don't have to do laundry so often."

Juan hid his smile. For someone with commitment issues, Jackson sure moved fast. "I'll bring some over tonight. You still good to hang at the festival tomorrow?"

"Yeah." Jackson pulled his green knitted cap over his ears. "I have the first shift at The Book Worm's booth, but after that, I'm good. You, me, and Mini-Boo are going to kick Jimmy's ass at the snowman contest."

They took care of Miss Mona and Onyx, then walked to the diner. Juan liked being a little closer to the center of town. Hobson Hills wasn't huge by any means—and the city limits stretched far past the actual town—but the heart of the town was the shops around Main street, and living so close to them was a treat.

"Jackson. Juan. What are you boys doing up so early? The sun isn't even out yet." Ines Torres watched them from her porch. Her small poodle, Sophia, sat at her feet.

"We're meeting Griff for breakfast, and he has an early shift," Jackson said. "Want me to bring you back something from the diner?"

Ines thought for a moment, eyes dancing in the streetlights. "Yes. Two omelets. Min-Jun is still sleeping, but he'll be hungry when he gets up."

Jackson wrinkled his nose. "I didn't need to know he stayed over, Ines."

Her laugh was full of sass. "We'll be family soon enough, cariño."

Jackson glared at her. "You better treat Grandpapa well, Abuela."

Ines grinned. "So fierce! I treat him very well, Jackson. You do the same for our Juan, yes?"

Jackson blushed. "Of course. He's my friend. We're very good friends, and we're going to meet our friend for breakfast." He turned and walked quickly past Ines's house.

Juan sighed and followed, waving goodbye to Ines. "We'll bring back your omelets. Feel free to bring Sophia over to nap with Miss Mona if it gets too loud today with all the little bits coming over."

Ines spent a good portion of every day babysitting Juan's friends' kids while they worked or ran errands. It could get a little wild sometimes, and Sophia was an older dog. She liked her peace and quiet.

"Thank you," she said, then grinned widely. "You might want to start closing the curtains or at least lowering the blinds."

Juan groaned and ran to catch up with Jackson.

Jackson took his hand. "Grandpapa loves her."

"I think she loves him too," Juan said, squeezing Jackson's mitten-covered fingers.

"If they get married, they'll be our neighbors," Jackson said, sounding both intrigued and horrified. "On one hand, Grandpapa makes the best kimchi, but on the other hand, I would know they were having sex right next door."

"Think about when you have kids though," Juan said, chuckling. "Babysitters right there."

"Hmm, good point."

They quickly made it to the diner and found Griff there, with Dean and Ray and a few of Jackson's brothers.

Griff saw them first and gave Jackson a mischievous smile. "Over here, guys."

Ray turned and saw Juan. His eyes narrowed into slits when he saw their joined hands, and Juan fought the urge to run. Ray was more protective than any alpha Juan knew, and the beta had a nasty right hook. *This may hurt.*

Dean watched his son with a small smile. "I hope you don't mind that we're joining you, baby boy. Jimmy got in last night and wanted one of Clairice's omelets. He doesn't believe us when we tell him they're better than Ray's."

"It's not possible," Jimmy said, watching Juan with a smirk. The pink streaks in his hair stood out under the bright lighting. "Hi, Juan. What a surprise! What brings you here today?"

Jules, Jackson's much younger brother, scrunched up his nose. "Juan is holding Jackson's hand, Jimmy. He was probably dragged here. Jackson always drags me to yard sales."

Jackson squeaked, then dropped Juan's hand like it was on fire. He pulled off his gloves and picked up his youngest brother, Jun. "Where's Jake? I'm surprised he's not here for breakfast."

Ray held a wiggling Min in his lap, but his glare stayed focused on Juan. "He's a lazy teenager now. He wanted to sleep in. Have a seat, Juan. Let's talk."

Jackson sat on Ray's other side. "Juan may have to get to work, Dad."

Ray melted a little at being called *Dad*, but then glared again at Juan. "He has time, don't you, Juan?"

Juan fought the urge to say *yes, sir* and sat beside Jackson.

Dean fought a grin. "How have you been, Juan?"

Jackson reached across the table and took Jimmy's warm cup of coffee. "How was school, Jimmy? You have… What? One semester left?"

"School's good, and I actually have three semesters left," Jimmy said, typing on his phone. "By the way, I have mono."

Jackson looked panicked and pushed Jimmy's cup back toward him. "Why didn't you say anything before I took a drink?"

Jimmy looked up and smiled innocently, picking up his cup. "Just kidding."

"Juan," Ray said, practically growling his name. "You didn't answer Dean's question."

He had to think a minute before he remembered the question. Jackson and his brothers were too distracting. "I've been good, thanks." *Keep it simple.*

"Anything you want to tell us?" Dean asked, tilting his head. "New jobs, annoying clients, a new boyfriend?"

Juan watched the panic spread across Jackson's face and sighed. "Nothing new to share. Jackson told me he gets to have a Mini-Boo day tomorrow."

Min giggled and bounced. "Jay Jay fun."

Jackson smiled and reached over to boop Min's nose. "You know it, Mini-Boo."

"Can we do a movie night Monday?" Jules asked, giving Jackson his best puppy dog eyes.

Jackson laughed. "Yeah. I got a couple of new ones."

The server arrived and took their orders, giving Juan a very brief reprieve from Ray's glare. She was just settling their drinks on the table in front of them when the door opened again, and Yeo ran through, looking disheveled and barely awake.

"Juan, oh my god!" Yeo hugged his head and squeezed uncomfortably tight. "Jimmy texted me."

"Sit down, Yeo," Dean said, snorting. "Juan was just telling us how he *isn't* dating anyone and how nothing new is going on at all."

Jackson sipped his coffee. "Yeo and Caden are trying for another baby."

Dean gasped and looked delighted. "Really?"

Yeo glared at Jackson. "We just started trying, so it might be a while."

"You need to make a new nursery?" Juan asked. Yeo was married to Carter's brother, Caden, so Juan knew they'd be the one doing any remodeling.

Yeo nodded. "We'll fix up one of the guestrooms."

They talked for a few minutes about babies, and Juan noticed Jackson squeezing Griff's hand. He'd have to make time to see if Griff needed any help setting up a nursery of his own.

Their food arrived and Jackson growled. "Griff, that's not enough food. You can't just eat oatmeal and grapefruit. Don't you want something more filling?"

Griff gave him a look. "Trust me. This is just fine."

"I'm making you dinner tonight," Jackson said, nodding once. "You need to eat more. It looks like you've lost a few pounds."

Ray watched the two men for a minute, confusion all over his face. Juan almost started laughing. He knew it looked like Griff and Jackson were a little more than just friends.

Juan ate his breakfast and watched Jun's smooshed face as the baby slept on Jackson's shoulder. Ray was going to be a pain in his ass, but the man sure made pretty babies.

SOMEHOW, Juan escaped Jackson's large family without any more pointed questions. While he didn't mind everyone in town knowing about them, Jackson definitely wasn't ready.

He was on his way to a job when his papa called. "Hey, Papa."

"Hi, Juan. Are you busy?" His papa sounded a little frazzled.

"Sure. What's up?"

"Oh, nothing important," Eduardo said. "I just wanted to check in on you. Your father wants to know if you're dating anyone yet."

"It hasn't even been a week since he asked, Papa," Juan said, sighing. "Ernie really is just a friend. He has his own alpha now anyway."

"Alright," Eduardo said, not sounding all that upset.

"Did you put your Christmas tree up yet?"

Juan laughed. "Now I see why you called."

"I sent you another box of ornaments. They're cute little foxes, and I couldn't resist getting them." Eduardo had always *loved* Christmas more than any other holiday. He always went overboard decorating and cooking. If Juan could put up with his dad a little better, he would fly to Arizona every year.

"I haven't been at my apartment much. I'll stop by and see if they're there," Juan said, smiling. He loved his papa.

"Haven't been spending time at home?" Eduardo's voice went high, and he giggled. "Where have you been sleeping, young man?"

Juan groaned. "You can't tell Dad, okay?"

"I promise," Eduardo said. "I know how your father gets. He has his notions and is as stubborn as a mule."

"He's name is Jackson, and I'm in love with him."

Eduardo squealed. "Juan, that's wonderful! He loves you too, right? Of course, he does. Who wouldn't love my baby boy?"

Juan smiled again. "I think he does, but his alpha grandfather and his alpha father were abusive. He's reluctant to trust an alpha, even though he knows me and we're good friends. I think it's giving up control, you know?"

"Oh, that poor boy," Eduardo said, voice sad. "I understand how he feels. Taking on an alpha means giving up part of yourself. He'd have to trust you completely."

"It doesn't have to mean giving up anything," Juan

said, frustrated. "I know how Dad thinks alphas and omegas work, but it's not like that all the time. I wouldn't want him to be anyone other than himself. Papa, if you could just meet him, you'd understand. He's like a mix of farm boy and hipster. He can be so practical one moment, then completely ridiculous and silly the next. I wouldn't want him to stifle that."

"I do love you, son," Eduardo said, sighing happily. "He's a lucky omega, and I'm sure he'll see it soon enough."

Juan pulled onto David and Sawyer's street. "I'm almost at my client's house."

"Okay," Eduardo said, still sounding a little dreamy. "I'll talk to you later. I'm sending some more ornaments too. For your omega."

The call ended, and Juan grinned as he parked the car next to Carter's van. The large Victorian in front of him was beautiful, but old. There always seemed to be something to fix on it.

Carter bumped his shoulder as they walked beside each other. "About time."

David met them at the door. The older man looked as attractive as usual in his skinny jeans, furry boots, and pink, oversized sweater. If David weren't happily married and Juan wasn't in love with a slightly neurotic omega, Juan would have been making a move on the man.

"Thank god, you two are here," David said, groaning. "I didn't realize the roof over the garage was in such bad shape or I would have had you guys do this in the summer instead of fucking winter."

Carter grinned and shrugged. "It's okay, David. You know we love you. Plus, Juan here is the one who's going on the roof. He owes me for stealing my van the other night."

Juan rolled his eyes. Like he wouldn't have made Carter work from the ground anyway. The man was good on his prosthesis, but he didn't need to be climbing all over an icy roof.

David smirked. "Was it Sunday night, by chance? You know that Joanie Lavender lives across the street from Jackson, right?"

Juan groaned.

"She saw some interesting things Sunday night," David said.

Carter started laughing. "Please tell me that means what I think it means."

"Shut up," Juan said, blushing. He pushed his friend toward his van. "Get the ladder and let's take care of this."

A little while later, Carter sent another box of shingles up their ladder hoist. Juan balanced on another ladder, trying to repair the broken shingles without climbing on the room. The shingles were icy, and it was a long way to the ground.

David and his teenage son, Ryder, stood behind Carter at the base of the ladder, both looking worried and holding their arms stretched out toward Juan, as if they could catch him if he fell.

"Be careful," David said. "Maybe we should wait. We can just put buckets under the leaking spots until spring."

"We don't fix it now, it'll get worse," Juan said, winking at Ryder. "It'll be alright."

"So, you and Jackson, huh?" Carter asked from the ground.

David snickered. "Don't startle him while he's up there, Carter."

Juan glared down at Carter. "We're dating, but we're not dating. Don't spread it around. Jackson's kinda wary of committing to an alpha. He doesn't need questions and teasing."

"Ray's going to kill you," Carter said, sounding pleased. "He loves Jackson like he was his own. I'll bring popcorn."

Ryder and David laughed.

Juan finished nailing one of the shingles down. "Do you think he'll really be that unhappy about Jackson choosing me?"

Carter grinned. "Do you even remember what you were like after we got home from each deployment?"

Juan winced. "I was young, damn it."

"Juan," David said, acting scandalized. "Did you chase all the pretty boys and girls?"

Carter laughed. "He was a manwhore."

"Juan seems really nice," Ryder said, shoving Carter. "Plus, aren't you guys best friends? He'll get over it if you treat Jackson well."

"Exactly," Carter said. "You just got to let him know you're ready to settle down. He knows you're a good guy, but Jackson is his son. He may trust you with his life, but the heart is a completely different thing."

CHAPTER 8

JACKSON

Jackson bounced Min on his hip as he waved goodbye to Cecilia, one of the teenagers that worked evenings at the bookstore. He was leaving a little late, but Jimmy had dropped Min off for him at the bookstore, so he wouldn't have to go by his papa's to pick him up.

"Are you ready for a fun sleepover, Mini-Boo? Then tomorrow, we'll go to the festival and build us a snowman, won't we?"

Min clapped and laughed. "Yes, yes. Stuffie time!"

Jackson laughed. "Oh, you're my favorite brother, Min. You *get* me."

Darkness fell quickly in the winter, but the streets were well-lit with both streetlights and Christmas lights. Min buried his face against Jackson's neck, his tiny nose a little ice cube.

Jackson walked faster, eager to get home to Juan. He knew his alpha would be there, even if they hadn't made any plans. Since their first night together, they had spent every waking minute together when they weren't working. Jackson fucking ached for Juan when he wasn't there. It was embarrassing as hell.

"I need to tell people we're together, Mini-Boo, but I'm scared," he whispered. "Juan deserves someone with a spine, doesn't he?"

"Juan nice," Min said.

"He's so much more than nice," Jackson said. "Did you know he insists on doing the dishes every night I cook? He says he can't cook for shit, but he can wash a pan. *He* wouldn't have done that, you know."

Jackson hated to even think about his alpha father. In his mind and heart, Ray Potts was his dad and would always be. The man who gave Jackson his damn eyes and freckles wasn't his father.

"Ray is a good daddy, isn't he?" Jackson asked.

"Love Daddy," Min agreed, giggling. "Love Papa, love G-papa, love Jay Jay, love Jimmy, love Jakey, love Julsie, love Yeo."

Jackson started laughing. "That's all of us but Jun."

Min wrinkled his nose. "Ju Ju stinky."

"Little brothers." Jackson nodded knowingly. "You'll get used to him, then he'll be your best friend. I didn't think I'd like Jimmy when he was born, but now he's at least a little more tolerable."

They turned onto his street, and Jackson felt a pang of guilt at the sight of all the pretty lights and decorations on his neighbors' houses. *I'm so lazy.*

"Mini-Boo, you don't like Christmas trees anyway, right?"

"Kissmiss, kissmiss, kissmiss!" Min started bouncing in his arms.

"Uh oh." Jackson really wished he had put a tree up. As he approached his house, he frowned, tilting his head. "Mini-Boo, is that my house?"

Someone had hung lights and garland under the front windows, and a string of colorful lights hung from the very top of the roof. A large green wreath with red and gold bows hung on the window and an inflatable reindeer stood next to the gate leading to the backyard.

Min clapped. "Pretty."

The door opened, and Juan gave him a nervous look before running his hands through hair. Hair that had a couple dark green streaks. "Do you like it?"

Jackson bit his lip, trying not to smile. "The house or your hair?"

Juan snorted. "Both, I guess."

Jackson walked up the steps and leaned up to kiss Juan. "I missed your green."

"I'll grow it out a bit for a faux hawk," Juan said, nipping Jackson's lip. "What about the house?"

"Pretty!" Min said, giggling and clapping.

"He is very pretty," Jackson nodded, agreeing.

Juan rolled his eyes and took Min from Jackson, tossing the toddler in the air and catching him. "I think you meant the house, Mini-Boo. Didn't you?"

Jackson peeked around him. "Shit, you did the whole house?"

Juan let him in, and Jackson grinned when he saw

all the decorations and the large tree. "It looks like Christmas threw up in here."

Miss Mona woofed, and Juan set Min down so the two could visit. Onyx sat at the top of the tree, surveying them from his perch.

"It's only a couple of weeks before Christmas," Juan said, turning toward the kitchen. "You can't drag your ass too long around here, Jackson."

I really, really can't. Some asshole omega will sweep him up, he thought.

Min finished getting his doggy kisses, then headed for the stairs. "Stuffie time!"

Jackson blushed and avoided Juan's curious look. "Can you make dinner while Min and I handle some business?"

Juan smirked. "Dinner's already made. I picked up pizza."

"Pizza," Min said happily, slowly climbing the stairs. "Stuffies first!"

Jackson sighed. "It's time. Please, follow me."

He picked Min up and carried him up the stairs to the guest room before setting him back down. His brother ran for the locked closet. "Stuffie time!"

Jackson pulled a key out of his pocket. "When I was a kid, I had one stuffie named Paul. He was a donkey. When Jimmy was around Min's age, I gave Paul to him. By then, *he* thought I was too old for toys." He unlocked the door and looked over his shoulder at Juan. "The problem is, I really like stuffed animals. They're like a big, fluffy, warm blanket of comfort and joy."

Juan blinked, looking confused. "Okay?"

"When I moved to Hobson Hills and started working for Yeo, I finally had privacy and spending money." Jackson opened the door. "This is my collection."

The closet was large and full of rows of stuffed animals. He had bears, lions, dogs, llamas, unicorns, and dragons. He was still debating on which penguin to buy to add to his collection.

Min squealed and ran inside, flopping down on the toys and rolling around. "Stuffie time! Jay Jay, play!"

Jackson didn't know what the expression on Juan's face meant. He knew a lot of adults liked stuffed animals, but it was probably kind of weird.

"Jay Jay!" Min sat up and glared at him. "Play."

Jackson shrugged and sat in the closet. Min climbed on his lap, and they started hugging and playing with the toys. He lost track of time as Min talked to him, sharing all his toddler secrets with Jackson's friends.

After a while, a throat clearing made him look up. Juan stood at the door with a soft look in his eyes. "Pizza is getting cold. You two need to go eat dinner."

Min yawned and clutched one of the stuffed bears. "Hungey."

Jackson jumped up and picked him up. "Will you take him down? I'll put everything away."

"You go on," Juan said. "I'll clean up."

Jackson eyed him suspiciously, then went downstairs. "He was bound to find out sometime, Mini-Boo. Better now than when we're married with nine children."

After dinner, Juan did dishes while Jackson gave

Min a bath and put him in the crib in the guestroom. "You're almost too big for the crib, aren't you? We'll have to get you a big boy bed."

Min yawned and hugged the knitted bear. Jackson had a feeling he'd lost another piece of his collection. He couldn't seem to make himself mind.

Jackson quietly shut the door behind him as he backed out of the room. He jumped a foot when he ran into a warm wall. Juan stood behind him.

"I fed the kids and let Miss Mona out. We're ready for bed," Juan said, dark eyes heating.

Jackson wrapped his arms around Juan's neck. "You're still here, so I'm assuming my secret didn't scare you away."

Juan shook his head. "I am a little pissed."

Jackson blinked. "Huh?" *Why would my odd collection make you angry?*

Juan pulled him into the bedroom, and Jackson stumbled, shocked to see all his stuffed toys arranged around the room.

"You shouldn't be hiding them away. They make you happy, and there's nothing for you to be ashamed of," Juan said, pulling him close. "Now that's settled, so kiss me."

Jackson laughed against his mouth. "Juan." *I love you.* He tried to say it, he really did.

"I know," Juan whispered, then kissed him, sliding his tongue alongside Jackson's.

Jackson melted against him, pushing and hopping as he tried to climb him. His ass was still a little sore from that morning, but damn if he didn't want his alpha again.

Juan picked him up and set him gently on the bed. "You know what I haven't gotten to do with you?"

Jackson pulled his shirt off and tossed it away. "I'm not into puppy play, Juan."

Juan snorted. "For fuck's sake, Jackson. I meant I haven't gotten to suck you off yet. Jesus!"

Jackson pushed his pants and underwear down, happy he had already taken his shoes off. "I'm really into that."

Juan shucked part of his own clothes and leaned over him, smiling as he kissed him. "You're obnoxious."

Juan kissed his way down Jackson's chest, taking his time to nip and suck each and every inch of him. By the time Juan made it to Jackson's stomach, he was covered in sweat and ready to fucking come.

Juan stroked Jackson's dick and licked the tip. "Fuck, you taste good." He rolled Jackson's balls in his palm, then swallowed his dick.

Jackson arched up. "Juan."

Juan ignored him and worked his mouth over Jackson's dick. When Jackson thought he was about to come, Juan would let up and eased his mouth away, slowing his strokes. Then, he'd start again, head bobbing over Jackson's dick.

"I'm going to murder you," Jackson panted. "Let me come."

Juan chuckled, and Jackson felt it reverberate through him. Finally, Juan worked him hard and kept his lips clamped around Jackson's dick when he came, swallowing every bit.

Jackson groaned as he flopped back. "Damn, that was good."

Juan gave him a satisfied smirk. "You make a nice desert, blue jay."

Jackson held his arms out. "Let's go to sleep."

Juan arched a brow. "Shouldn't we shower first? You're covered in sweat."

Jackson scowled. "I'm fucking glistening, asshole."

"I'll wash your back," Juan said, wiggling his brows.

Jackson started laughing. "Okay, but you have to change the sheets too."

A few hours after falling asleep, Jackson woke up suddenly, unsure of what he was hearing.

"No," Juan said, voice shaky and thick with tears. "Dyl, fuck. Dyl, your face."

Jackson sat up and watched Juan roll back and forth, clearly locked in a bad dream. His alpha's face was covered in agony and tears poured down his cheeks.

Jackson felt his own tears well. He had heard Juan talk at their Dolly's Diamonds and Dragons meetings. He knew he still had dreams about his time overseas. He hadn't realized how it would feel to see it happening.

Jackson wiped his eyes and gripped Juan's shoulder, shaking him. "Juan, I need you to wake up. Now." He tried to keep his voice soft, but firm.

Juan pushed him away, practically growling. "Don't be an idiot, Julio."

Jackson shook him again. "Juan, wake up."

It took a few tries, but Juan finally opened his eyes, groggy and out of it. "Jackson? Fuck, I'm sorry."

Jackson draped himself over Juan, pressing his head against Juan's chest. "No need to be sorry, Juan. Tell me how to help."

He felt Juan wipe a hand down his face and shudder. "I'm sorry. I can go home."

Jackson frowned. "You are home. Now, how do I help? Do you want to talk about it?"

"No," Juan said, almost yelling. "No, I don't want to remember it. Tell me about the bookstore, blue jay. Please?"

Jackson leaned up and kissed his chin. "Okay. So, I've been taking accounting classes so I can help Yeo with the books, and I kind of like bookkeeping. Yeo's been giving me more responsibility over purchasing inventory too. He likes to spend his time finding expensive and rare collectables and selling them online. I hate to admit it, but that brings in almost a third of what the rest of the store does."

Jackson talked about work, then Luke and Griff, for an hour before Juan fell back to sleep. Jackson stayed draped across him and propped his chin on Juan's shoulder.

I need to up my game. Juan needs me.

JUAN AND MIN waited for Jackson on a bench near The Book Worm's booth at the Winter Festival. Jackson smiled as he watched Min wave his little arms and talk Juan's ear off.

"Son, I think we need to talk."

Jackson spun around, wincing when he saw his papa. Dean had Jun in the baby carrier strapped to his chest. Jackson's youngest brother was bundled up in a red snow suit, mittens, and hat. He grinned at Jackson and waved one of his arms.

"Did you need something, Papa?" Jackson asked.

"I need you to tell me what's going on with you and Juan." Dean gave him a pointed look. "It wasn't even two weeks ago that you told me you would never date an alpha."

"We're not dating," Jackson said automatically, then winced.

"Do you go places together?" Dean asked, raising a brow.

"Yes," Jackson said, mumbling.

"Do you have romantic dinners, kiss and/or fuck?" Dean asked, grinning.

"Papa," Jackson whined, squeezing his eyes shut. "Don't make me say it."

"You're dating the man," Dean said, nodding. "You don't have to say it until you're ready, baby boy, but I need to know if it's serious. I know Juan. Ray is pissed at him right now, but he's been worried because Juan's been sad lately."

"I keep him plenty happy," Jackson said, glaring. "He smiles and laughs with me, and we talk all the time."

"As well as kiss and/or fuck?" Dean asked, smirking.

Jackson groaned. "Yes, Papa. We kiss *and* fuck."

"Are either of you seeing other people?" Dean asked, tone serious.

"No," Jackson said, scowling. "He better not even look at another person."

Dean tilted his head. "Alright. Now, I know. Ray will threaten to kick his ass and scowl for a while, but you'll bring Juan to dinner Sunday nights. He's also coming with you to Christmas breakfast."

"Yes, sir," Jackson said, trying to decide if he was happy or annoyed. On one hand, he wanted Juan with him all the time. On the other hand, he hated being told what to do. It made his eye twitch.

Yeo popped up beside Dean. "Your shift's over, Jackson." Yeo's eyes danced. "Your boyfriend is waiting."

Jackson sniffed. "I can't believe you're the oldest."

He left them behind and went to Juan's bench. Juan stood and smiled. "Are you ready for fun? Min said he wants to go on a sleigh ride."

Jackson wrapped his hands around one of Juan's arms and cuddled into his side. "That sounds like a good idea. By the way, Harper said you helped him with the design for our booth."

Juan smiled smugly. "Yeah. I did most of it."

Jackson snorted. "He said you handed him the tools and told him what to carve."

"Like I said, I did most of it."

They waited in line for the sleigh. Harper's ponies were pulling it, and this year, Harper's cousin Janelle was stuck with driving duty.

When they were finally settled in the sleigh with

blankets covering their legs and Min wedged between them, Jackson brought up Juan's nightmare.

"Are you sure you don't want to talk about your dream last night?" he asked.

Juan winced. "No. Absolutely not. I'm fucking mortified you had to see that."

Jackson shook his head. "I'm glad I was there, Juan. It kills me to think of you having to go through that alone. We don't have to talk about the dreams, but I *will* be there for you when you have them."

Juan started to say something, then closed his mouth. Finally, he took a deep breath. "My dad isn't a bad guy, but you know what he's like."

Jackson nodded. "You talk about him a lot at our Dolly's Diamonds and Dragons meetings."

"When I didn't re-enlist after that last deployment, I went to stay with them for a few months while I figured out what I was going to do. He was pissed I didn't re-enlist, and then, I woke him up with one of my nightmares. Most of the time I just… you know, but sometimes I scream."

"It's okay to cry," Jackson said, frowning. "You were remembering something traumatic. It's okay to feel."

"Dad was disgusted," Juan said quietly. "He said it was a good thing I wasn't in the army anymore since I wasn't a man."

Jackson growled. "It's *a good thing* the asshole lives in a different state."

Juan laughed, voice breaking. "I know he's full of shit, but sometimes the things he's told me all my life linger in my head. It's hard to talk about this stuff.

That's why I like our Dolly club. We can talk or not, and it's not a big thing."

"I don't want you to feel like you have to talk to me," Jackson said. "I just want you to know you can. This thing we're doing, it's important. *You're* important. I want to get it right."

Juan leaned over and kissed him. "We will, blue jay. We'll figure this shit out."

"Shit," Min said suddenly. "Shit bad word."

Jackson winced. "It is, Mini-Boo. Sorry we say a lot of bad words."

"Daddy get mad at you."

Juan shrugged. "Daddy is already mad at me."

"Speaking of Dad," Jackson said, smiling widely. "He's waiting for us."

Ray stood at the small loading platform. His arms were crossed and he scowled.

"Daddy!" Min said, giggling and holding his arms out. "Love you."

Ray melted and pulled his son from the sleigh. "Love you too, Mini-Boo. Come here, sweetheart."

Juan held his arms out. "I love you too, Daddy."

Ray's eyes narrowed into slits. "Jackson, hold Min while I kill my bastard best friend."

Jackson smiled. "Okay." He took Min and started walking away.

"Blue jay," Juan yelled, starting to run when Ray cracked his knuckles. "You're abandoning me?"

Ray growled and chased after him while the people around them laughed.

"We need hot cocoa," Jackson yelled back. "Sorry,

boo."

He got some cocoa and found them a nice spot near the pond. People were ice skating while holiday music played from a covered sound system nearby.

Jackson sipped his cocoa and watched Juan dodge Ray to hide behind Gramps and Grammy Wilson. "Well, Mini-Boo, my alpha can sure run."

"Why is Juan running from your dad?" Griff asked, sitting beside them.

His daughter Bea smiled and waved at Min. They were about the same age. Jackson arranged the toddlers between them, and the two immediately leaned toward each other, giggling.

Jackson leaned over to hug his friend. "You got today off? I thought you had to work."

"Another nurse needed more hours, and I wanted to take Bea to her first Winter Festival," Griff said, yawning. "So, Juan and Ray are fighting?"

Jackson watched Juan crawl around The Irish Rose's booth while Ray looked around the crowds, searching for him. "I think I may be dating Juan."

Griff grinned. "I think you are."

"How's Luke and Britney doing?" he asked. "I've been wrapped up in Juan the past few days."

Griff rolled his eyes and scowled. "Everything was going well until his parents found out."

"What happened?" Jackson asked worriedly. "I haven't heard from him the last couple of days."

"They fired him," Griff said, shaking his head. "He sells more cars at their stupid dealership than any of the other salespeople, plus he's their son, but they fired him. They told him he could come back if he stopped all his talk about my baby being his."

"Poor Luke," Jackson said, shoulders slumping. *I'm a shitty boyfriend and a shitty friend.*

"He'll figure things out," Griff said. "Britney is a whole other story. The woman actually came to me and told me she would *step aside* for me and the baby. Do you know how hard it was to convince her there is no way in hell I'll marry Luke?"

"Wow, that's harsh." Luke's voice came from behind them.

Jackson looked over his shoulder and grinned. Luke and Britney were bundled up and holding hands.

He patted the bench beside him. "Have a seat. We're watching my big, brave alpha run from my dad."

Luke sat and pulled Britney on his lap. "Is that Juan hiding behind Harper and Grey's chairs?"

"It is," Jackson said. "I didn't know he folded up that easily. Fucker takes up two thirds of the bed."

Luke laughed, then sobered. "Griff told you?"

"Yeah," Jackson said, patting Luke's knee. "They're assholes, and they don't deserve you."

"No, they don't," Britney said and kissed Luke. "My man is moving in with me and Nana. He'll find a better job, and they'll regret losing him."

Jackson smiled, thinking of the family around him. Luke and Griff would make good dads to both Bea and the new baby. If things went the way he thought they would, Britney would be a good mom to them too.

"You're a good alpha, Luke," Jackson said. "There are a lot of good alphas around here."

Griff nodded. "There are. One of them just crawled under Carter's table. Oh no, Carter just grabbed him and is calling Ray over."

Jackson sighed. "Come on, Mini-Boo. I have to go save my man."

Min clapped. "Bea come too."

Jackson handed his cup to Griff and slung a giggling toddler over each shoulder. "If you insist."

He jogged past one of the cheesy carnival games and a large penguin caught his eye. It was so round and its cheeks puffed out. *That's my penguin.* He hurried to where Juan, Carter, and Ray were. Noah stood between them, trying to be the voice of reason.

"Ray, you know Juan's a good guy and Jackson wants him," Noah said. "I think. I don't know Jackson that well. I assume he wouldn't date Juan if he didn't want him."

Jackson groaned. So much for the voice of reason. "Gentlemen," he said, looking between Ray and Juan. "Clearly we have a problem here."

"I just need to hit him a few times, Jackson," Ray said, signing for Noah's benefit. "I'll feel better after that."

"I thought you didn't like fighting," Noah said, narrowing his eyes.

"This is my son we're talking about," Ray said, frowning. "Juan shouldn't be fooling around with my Jackson."

Carter tsked. He stood with his arms wrapped around Juan. "It's shameful. I mean, Juan saved your life how many times? Three, right? Then, you know he's an honest, hardworking guy. That's just not the kind of person Jackson needs."

Jackson grinned, then handed Min to Ray and Bea to Noah. "I understand this is a pride thing or something like that, but you can't pummel each other. Bad example and all that shit. You can, however, compete at the third booth down from us. There's a penguin I need. Now, is my boyfriend or my dad gonna get it for me?"

CHAPTER 9

JUAN

Juan grinned as he pulled on his warm clothing. Jackson was still asleep and was curled around the giant stuffed penguin Juan had won him yesterday. The second, far inferior even if it was identical, giant penguin sat in a chair in front of the window. Ray and he had spent way too much money to win those damn penguins.

Fucking rigged carnival games.

Juan leaned over and kissed Jackson's head. His omega had today off but planned on spending it Christmas shopping with his brothers. Juan and his friends had their own plans.

He fed Miss Mona and Onyx, then fixed Miss Mona's bangs into a topknot with a pink scrunchie. "Who's the prettiest girl in the whole world?"

Miss Mona woofed.

"You bet it's you," Juan said and kissed her head.

A twenty-minute drive later, he turned and drove down the long, bumpy driveway to Reuben's secluded cabin. Ernie kept motion detector cameras out there and he had seen something.

He parked behind one of the other vehicles and went inside.

Ernie had a map spread out on the small kitchen table. He looked up and grinned. "Glad you could make it. I think we're going to get him today."

"Are you sure we shouldn't wait until nighttime?" Mateo asked. "Sasquatch are nocturnal."

"Yeah, but, they don't, like, disappear during the day," Artie said. The young man was visiting Mateo's family for the winter break. He was a believer, so he'd been invited on their Bigfoot excursion.

"Also, Reuben doesn't want me exploring the forests in December at night," Ernie said, rubbing his slight baby bump. "He says it's not good for the baby or his sanity."

"Smart man," Carter said. He was stretched out on the couch with his feet propped in Noah's lap. Juan's two friends were *not* believers, but they did make handy packhorses.

Juan leaned over the couch. "Did you look over the plans I sent you?"

Carter grinned. "Will Jackson let you do it?"

"I think so," Juan said. "Right now, the attic is wasted space. It's well insulated and has a private staircase already leading to it."

"What are we waiting for?" Ernie said, impatient. "We have to find Bigfoot."

"Someone's grumpy," Carter said.

Ernie growled. "I have an alpaca living in my house. I can be grumpy if I want."

Juan started laughing. "Reuben finally talked you into letting Peppermint inside?"

"For two hours a day," Ernie said, rolling his eyes. "The rest of my herd is gonna get jealous, then he'll want to schedule two hours for each of them." He looked around the room, exasperated. "Now, what the hell is taking so long?"

"We're just waiting for one more person," Mateo said, grinning at Juan. "Do you want to hide under the table when he gets here?"

Juan groaned. "Can't we just forget yesterday?"

"The entire town saw, man," Artie said, laughing. "I don't think anyone is forgetting."

"I took pictures," Carter said. "It was beautiful."

"It's not fair," Ernie said, stomping his foot. "I missed everything just because I wanted Zoe's damn cinnamon rolls."

Juan heard the crunch of tires on snow and looked outside. "Ray brought Gramps too. Good. Gramps has a lot of experience with the local terrain."

The two men came in, and Ray punched his arm when he walked past him. "Juan."

Juan grinned and nodded. "Daddy."

Ray growled and went to grab him, and Gramps put an arm around his shoulders.

The older man chuckled. "You two are worse than teenagers. Now, let's see this image you caught, Ernie."

Ernie nodded enthusiastically. "Here it is." He handed it to Gramps. "You can see the dark shape next to the bush, right? That's too big to be a rabbit or a raccoon."

Gramps squinted. "Well, yes, but it could be any number of things. It could be a small bear, or a fox, or a coyote. Hell, it could be a wild pig."

"That's why we need to investigate it," Juan said, nodding. "It *could* be a baby Bigfoot."

Carter sat up and groaned. "Alright. Let's get this over with. Then I can go home and try to find where Elijah hid my Christmas present."

They loaded all their gear onto Carter and Noah, then headed out. Ray and Gramps led the way. Somehow, Juan ended up in the back with Ernie.

"Hey," Ernie whispered. "I know Ray is worried about you breaking Jackson's heart, but are you sure he won't break yours?"

Juan gave him a surprised look. "You're the first to ask. Honestly, I trust him not to purposefully hurt me, and I'm not going to give him any reason to hate me."

"So, you're saying you two will be fine because nothing's going to rock the boat?" Ernie asked, arching a brow.

Juan thought about it. "He's seen me at my worst and was okay with it. I know just about everything about him. I think we'll be alright. I just need to give him time to see he can trust me. Fuck, we just started this thing a week ago."

Ernie's smile was sweet. "Sometimes a week can be an eternity, Juan. Sometimes a year can seem like seconds. Don't worry about time. Instead, do things when they feel right."

"This is the spot, right?" Ray asked from the front.

Ernie looked around. "Yes. Look for prints."

Juan looked around the small clearing but froze when he heard a whine. He dropped to his knees and looked under the nearest bush. A pair of sad brown eyes met his.

"Hey, buddy," Juan said softly.

Ernie gasped and dropped down beside him. "Is it Bigfoot?"

"Nope." Juan held his hand out, and the dog sniffed it. "It's a cute, fuzzy mutt."

Ernie chuckled and held his own hand out. "Hey there, cutie."

The dog had long, matted brown fur and brown eyes. Its two front paws were white.

It licked first Juan's hand, then Ernie's.

"Come on out, buddy," Juan said. The dog slowly slid out from under the bush and crawled into Juan's lap. It shook, and Juan hugged it tightly. "The poor thing is so cold."

Gramps patted his shoulder. "We better get Bigfoot to Doc Grover. He'll check him over and clean him up."

"Well, this didn't go as planned, but at least we know no Sasquatch were here," Ernie said, disappointed.

Carter grumbled the whole way back to the cabin. "You guys can do this yourself next time. I swear I'm not coming."

Noah laughed. "You said that last time."

About three hours later, they knew Bigfoot was a boy and relatively healthy. The staff at the veterinary office had given the puppy a bath and some food and water.

"He's still a puppy, but he'll probably be pretty big," Dr. Grover said. "Just by looking, I'd say he has some German Shepard and Collie blood in him. He needs several good meals and a warm bed. He must not have been out there for long or he'd have frozen to death."

"Does he have a chip?" Ernie asked. All the guys sat in the waiting room.

"Nope," Doc said. "He doesn't have any tags either. We'll keep him for a week to fully check him over, neuter him, and give him his shots, but then he'll need a home."

They all looked at Juan.

"I live in an apartment," he said, holding his hands up. "What about Carter?"

"Elijah will make him live in the barn if he brings another pet home," Gramps said, chuckling.

Carter nodded. "He's not wrong."

"We have enough already," Ray said, shaking his head. "Don't look at me."

"So do we," Mateo said, looking a little sad. "Bigfoot is so cute though."

Noah shook his head too. "I have the horses to take care of."

Artie was next. "I live on campus, man. They won't let me bring a dog."

Ernie gave them all a happy look. "I'll take him."

"No," they all said together.

"You have two babies and another on the way,"

Gramps said, rubbing Ernie's back. He looked at Juan. "Now, do you *really* live in an apartment?"

JUAN SHOWED JACKSON ANOTHER PICTURE. "Look at him here. This is right after they gave him his bath. Look at that tongue. I can't believe we have to wait until next week to bring him home."

Jackson sighed, and Juan put his phone down. He really hadn't thought Jackson would be upset about Bigfoot, but maybe he was pushing things.

Jackson took his hand. "I want to have your babies."

Juan blinked. "Okay?"

Jackson tilted his head. "Is that weird? That's weird. Okay, so I'll rephrase. You're the sweetest alpha I know, and I want to have your babies. There. That's not weird, right?"

Juan grinned. "Not at all."

"Miss Mona," Jackson said, and the dog came in from the kitchen, head cocked. "You're getting a little brother."

"Woof."

"Brothers can be a pain, but in the long run, they're worth it," Jackson said. "Onyx?" He looked around. Onyx watched them from the top of the Christmas tree. "You're also getting a baby brother. Don't terrorize him more than is needed, alright?"

"I'm really glad I build a fortified tree stand," Juan said, watching Onyx. "Has he even left the tree since we got it?" His phone rang, interrupting their very important conversation. "Hey, Papa."

"Juan," Eduardo said, voice thick with tears. "I have some bad news."

"Papa? What's wrong?" He stood and started pacing the floor. Jackson watched from the couch, worry covering his face.

"He didn't tell me," Eduardo said. "He didn't say anything."

"About what? Is it Dad? What didn't he say?"

"He's dying. Cancer," Eduardo said. "It's bad. The doctors don't think he'll live more than a few days."

Juan didn't even notice when he sat on the floor. Miss Mona whined and curled up beside him, and Onyx was suddenly there in his lap. Jackson's arms were around him, and his papa was still talking.

"He refused treatment," Eduardo said, voice shaking. "He knew months ago, and he refused treatment. He didn't want to be weak. He didn't tell anyone. None of the men at work or his friends at the bar. He didn't tell me."

"He's dying? They know that for sure? It's not a mistake?" Juan asked.

"He collapsed at work," Eduardo said. "From pain. His organs are shutting down, and there's nothing they can do."

Juan couldn't speak. He couldn't think. He didn't want to lose his dad. They didn't get along well, but he was always there in the background. A steady presence that adored and pampered Juan's papa and bossed Juan and Lucía around.

Jackson took the phone. "Hi, Mr. Vega. This is Juan's friend, Jackson. Please tell me where you are. I'll book us flights right away."

After a while, Juan noticed his back was hurting and his ass was numb. He was still sitting on the floor. Jackson's head was on his shoulder.

"Dad's dying," Juan said, choking on the words.

"I booked two tickets to Arizona," Jackson said. "Jimmy is going to come watch the house, and Carter and Yeo know we'll both be out of town for a little bit."

Juan felt the tears fall, but he still couldn't move. "I know you don't want to hear it, but I love you, Jackson."

"I love you too," Jackson said softly. "I didn't want it, but damn me if it's not the scariest and most beautiful thing I'll ever feel."

"Papa said he knew he had cancer but refused the treatments," Juan said. "He said he didn't want to be weak. He didn't want to *look* weak."

Jackson didn't say anything.

"How could he? How could he not fight?" Juan asked. "He loves Papa. How could he choose to leave him instead of fucking looking weak?"

"I don't know," Jackson said softly. "I'm so sorry, Juan."

Juan's mind felt numb and fuzzy. He didn't want to think. He didn't want to do anything.

"I'm going to start packing, okay? If you need me, yell." Jackson hugged him one more time, then stood.

Fuck, he felt cold. He wanted Jackson beside him.

Jackson gave him a worried look. "Fuck it. I can't

just leave you sitting here." He sat back down and typed a message on his phone before hugging Juan again. "I wish I could make this better for you."

A few moments later, Min-Jun and Ines came in the backdoor. Ines saw his face and joined the pile on the floor, wrapping her arms around them.

"I'll pack your bags," Min-Jun said but paused to lean down and kiss Juan's head. "Take your time to feel."

Juan didn't know what that was supposed to mean, but he appreciated Min-Jun's care. He held onto Jackson and hoped tomorrow would be better.

CHAPTER 10

JACKSON

The red-eye flight to Arizona was surprisingly fast despite the two stops along the way. Jackson wasn't ready when the plane landed. Juan didn't look much better. His alpha was so quiet and spaced out.

He knew Juan had issues with his dad, but he had underestimated how much Juan looked up to the man. This was killing him.

A young Hispanic woman met them at the gate. She started crying when she saw Juan and ran to hug him. *This must be Lucía,* Jackson thought.

Juan seemed to transform in front of them. He had his cocky grin back in place and didn't seem to have a care in the world. *My poor alpha.*

Juan wrapped his arms around her. "It'll be okay, brat."

"It doesn't seem real. What's Papa going to do? He lives to take care of Dad." Lucía buried her face against Juan's shoulder.

"We'll figure it all out," Juan said, eyes meeting Jackson's.

Jackson nodded and gave him a sad smile. He didn't know what the hell he was supposed to do. He just wanted to be there for Juan and help him through this.

Lucía seemed to notice him for the first time. "Oh shit! Is this Jackson?" She wiped at her eyes and nose. "I'm not making a good first impression."

Jackson rolled his eyes and pulled her into a hug of his own. "Forget it. You have nothing to prove to me. Besides, Juan already told me you were a brat."

She scowled and punched Juan's arm. "Brothers are the worst."

"Oh, let me tell you all about mine," Jackson said. "First, one of my younger brothers named a donkey after me."

Lucía laughed. "Seriously?"

"Yes," Jackson said. "The rest of the family decided that was okay, and Jackson the donkey is a family pet."

Jackson kept up with the stories as they left the airport. Fortunately, with six brothers, he could entertain her for a while. Juan just smiled through it all, wearing his no-cares-at-all alpha mask.

By they time they reached the nice two-story in Mesa, Lucía was a little more settled, and Jackson had discovered he really liked the woman. She had a sense of humor and loved her brother. How could he not like her?

An older Hispanic omega stood on the front steps. He looked a complete mess with red-rimmed eyes and disheveled clothing.

"They wouldn't let me stay the night," the man said, wringing his hands. "I can't go back for three more hours."

Juan ran to his papa and hugged him. "You need to eat and rest, Papa. We'll go see Dad together during visiting hours, alright?"

Juan pulled his papa inside, and Jackson squeezed Lucía's hand before following. Juan's childhood home was simple and tidy. There weren't a lot of decorations, but those they had were tasteful. When compared to his own cluttered home, Jackson kind of wondered what Juan saw in him.

There were only a few Christmas decorations around the room, and while the tree was large, it was sparsely decorated. *I thought Juan said his papa loved Christmas decorations.*

"Oh, I'm so sorry," Eduardo said and tried to compose himself. "You must be Jackson."

Jackson nodded and hugged the man back. "It's nice to meet you, Mr. Vega. I'm sorry this is how it happened, but I'm glad to be here with Juan."

Eduardo smiled sadly. "Me too. Come in, and let me show you his baby pictures."

"Papa!" Juan said, scowling when Lucía laughed.

Jackson ignored him and went to the living room with Eduardo. "I *need* to see a little bitty Juan."

Lucía smirked. "Can't you do that every night?"

Jackson snickered when Juan yanked her ponytail. Eduardo sat him on the couch and pulled one of the three photo albums from the nearly empty book shelf. Jackson could have fit at least fifty books on that shelf.

"Juan looks just like his father," Eduardo said and sat beside Jackson. He flipped to the very first page. "Look at them."

On the left was a faded picture of a two-year old. "That's his dad?"

"Yes," Eduardo said, smoothing a hand over it. "The one on the right is Juan."

"They could be twins," Jackson said, laughing at the picture of Juan with a cowboy hat and boots. He was perched on a wooden rocking horse. "I didn't know you were a cowboy, Juan."

Juan groaned and sat beside him, wrapping his arm around Jackson's shoulders. "I was also an astronaut, a spy, and a space pirate."

"I'm dating such a well-rounded man," Jackson said, pressing a hand to his heart. "My papa must be so proud."

Eduardo showed him more pictures of Juan and Lucía as children, and before he knew it, they had looked through all three albums, and Jackson had so much ammunition against the two younger Vegas.

Juan rubbed his face against the top of Jackson's head. "I order you to forget everything you just heard. Okay?"

"Because I love you, I'll forget what I heard," Jackson said. "But I can't forget what I saw. You had such a cute baby tush."

Eduardo stood. "I'll make us some breakfast before we go. Jackson, do you have any preferences?"

"Why don't you visit with Juan while I make breakfast?" Jackson asked. "You have to be worn out."

Eduardo looked surprised. "Oh, thank you."

Jackson left Juan with his papa and sister and went to inspect the kitchen. Unlike the rest of the house, it was cluttered with knickknacks and cookbooks. Jackson ran his fingers over the small portrait of Dolly Parton that hung over the small radio on the counter.

He grinned. *This is Eduardo's room.*

He turned the radio on, and a Dolly Parton song filled the air. "A Coat of Many Colors" was one of Mrs. Odell's favorites. He hummed along and quickly made some French toast.

He was putting the last plate on the table when arms wrapped around his waist. "Thank you, blue jay."

Jackson leaned back in Juan's arms. "I like your papa and sister."

He felt Juan's smile against his neck. "They like you."

"I packed one of mine and Min's favorite hugging stuffies," Jackson whispered. "If you need to, you can sleep with it tonight. Okay?"

"You're my favorite hugging stuffie," Juan said. "But thank you."

"I wish I could do more for you," Jackson said, sighing.

"You're here. That's the best thing you could do," Juan said. "Now, let's eat breakfast. I'm starving."

The conversation stayed light through the meal, but Eduardo started to droop when it was time to leave. Jackson took his hand and squeezed it. He didn't know what he would do without Juan and they'd only been together for a little over a week, not thirty-six years.

They all piled into Lucía's car and drove to the hospital.

A young man in a business suit met them there. Lucía's fiancé, Manuel, looked exhausted. "You must be Juan and Jackson." They shook his hand while Eduardo went to check in.

"Dad's room is this way," Lucía said. They followed her to the room and found Eduardo speaking with the doctor outside the door.

Juan's papa sobbed, and Juan pulled him close. "What's the news?"

"We're making him as comfortable as we can, but he's fading fast," the doctor said. "I don't expect him to last through the day. I'm so sorry."

Juan hugged his papa and held him as he sobbed. Manuel did the same with Lucía. Jackson didn't know what to do. He settled his hand on Juan's back and felt some of his alpha's tension drain under his fingers. *Oh, Juan.*

After a few minutes, they were allowed in the room, and Jackson choked back a sob of his own. The man looked like an older version of Juan, and Jackson hated it. It made it harder to keep his own emotions under control.

"Juan?" Jorge's voice was strained.

"Dad." Juan pulled Jackson to his dad's bedside. "This is Jackson, my omega."

Jackson wanted to make some joke about being his own omega, but Jorge looked so pleased, and, well, Jackson called Juan his alpha all the time. "Hi."

"My son will be a good alpha for you," Jorge choked out.

"He will," Jackson readily agreed. He wouldn't be the kind of alpha Jorge thought he ought to be, but he would be the alpha Jackson wanted and needed.

Jackson patted Juan's back. "I'll go get everyone some coffee."

Juan gave him a grateful smile, and he left the room, Manuel slipping out with him.

Lucía's fiancée gave him a sad smile. "We'll give them some time, yes?"

CHAPTER 11

JUAN

Not long after Jackson and Manuel left, Jorge gave Juan a look. "I need to speak to Juan alone," he said, stumbling over the words.

"We'll wait outside," Eduardo said and steered Lucía toward the door. "Take your time."

Juan didn't want to be there. He didn't want to see his dad like this. The man had always been larger than life – brash and loud. Now, there were so many tubes hooked into him, and he looked almost withered.

"I'm glad you came," Jorge said, and Juan felt a surge of guilt. He hadn't been to visit in a while. "Your omega looks good. Take care of him, Juan."

"I will," he said gruffly. "Jackson's a good guy. We've been friends for a while."

"Omegas and alphas aren't friends," Jorge said. "There are things an alpha can't share with an omega, especially his own omega."

"Jackson and I aren't like that." Juan shook his head. He shouldn't be arguing with his dad like this.

"A man needs to *be* a man, Juan. Omegas aren't happy if they don't have an alpha to guide them. It's your duty as an alpha."

Juan couldn't help but laugh. "I think Jackson would neuter me if I tried to *guide* him."

Jorge choked out his own laugh. "He looks so sweet."

"He is," Juan said, grinning. "But there's a good amount of spice in him too."

"Your papa was like that," Jorge said, eyes shining, "before we married."

"Papa?"

"Yes," Jorge said, nodding. "He liked to dance and sing. He had a wild way about him that I hate to admit I miss. When we got married, I helped him settle down. We trimmed away all that wildness."

Juan gritted his teeth. There was no use arguing with the man now.

"I know you're different than me," Jorge said, startling Juan. "You don't see things like I do, and that's alright. Different isn't always wrong. I wish I had understood that sooner."

"It's okay, Dad," Juan said, swallowing hard. "I know you love me."

"I do," Jorge said, eyes softening. "You, Lucía, and Eduardo are the joy of my life. I know I'm leaving this world something special."

Juan barely held his tears back. He never thought his dad would talk like this.

"I remember when you were in fourth grade, and the Baxter boy next door was picking on that young omega down the street." Jorge chuckled and it sounded painful. "You kicked his ass, and you were three years younger. You always protected people. That's why I thought you'd do well in the army."

"I did," Juan said, "For a long time."

"I never joined up," Jorge said. "I thought about it, but my dad needed me for the construction company."

Juan stayed silent. He'd heard all about his dad's dreams of being a military hero.

"I don't know what happened to you over there," Jorge said. "I don't understand it, but I wish I had tried harder to listen to you. I'm sorry, son."

Juan squeezed his dad's hand. "I love you, Dad."

Jorge smiled softly. "I'm glad. I've been hard on you and Lucía."

"We made it," Juan said, giving his dad a half-hearted smile.

"You did." Jorge patted his hand. "I need you to promise me something."

"Anything."

"Eduardo is going to have a hard time with this. We've been together so long, and he relies on me." Jorge looked conflicted for a moment. "I haven't always been the man he deserves."

"You adore him," Juan said. Even if his dad was controlling and too traditional, there was no doubt in Juan's mind that he loved Juan's papa.

"I do," Jorge said, breathing heavily, "but I'm also selfish."

Juan shook his head. His dad picked a damn fine

time to finally try some introspection. "What do you need me to do?"

"Do you remember when you were young and the two of you would dance in the kitchen?" Jorge asked.

"Yeah." Juan also remembered the day Jorge told him to grow up and stop acting like a ballerina.

"Eduardo loves to dance, but I wouldn't dance with him," Jorge said. "I can't dance for the life of me, and I didn't want people to laugh. I didn't even want him to know I couldn't do it."

"Dad," Juan said, groaning. "That's so fucking stupid."

Jorge snorted. "I know that now. I want you to dance with him again. Don't let me ruin that anymore."

Juan rubbed his eyes, then nodded. "I can do that. I think Papa is stronger than you think, Dad. He'll be okay. I'll make sure of it."

"Thank you," Jorge said, closing his eyes for a moment. "Can you send Lucía in? I need to talk to her too."

"Yes," Juan said and stood. He leaned over and kissed his father's forehead. "I love you, Dad. You're a stubborn, old-fashioned bastard, but I love you."

Jorge laughed. "I love you too, son."

Juan left and waved Lucía through the door. "Your turn, brat."

She elbowed him on the way in and shut the door behind her.

Eduardo stood there, alone, shoulders slumped. Juan smiled softly and pulled his papa into his arms and started to sway. He hummed his favorite song, Dolly Parton's "Love is Like a Butterfly."

His papa laughed and settled his head on Juan's shoulder. "It's been a long time since we danced."

"I missed it," Juan said. "I've missed you, Papa."

They swayed and sang the lyrics softly while people walked past, going and coming from the other rooms on the floor.

Juan felt Jackson's eyes on him eventually and turned his head, meeting his omega's gaze. Jackson grinned and swayed, practically bouncing in place to see him dancing with his papa again. *Damn, I love that man*, he thought. *My hipster farm boy in his flannel shirts and UGGs.*

A few moments later, Lucía came out of the room, wiping her eyes on her sleeve. She went straight to Manuel. "Papa, he wants to see you."

Eduardo leaned up and kissed Juan's cheek. "Thank you, my sweet boy." He left them in the hallway.

Jackson handed him a cup of coffee. "This disgusting black tar will keep you going a little longer."

"Thanks, blue jay." Juan pulled him in for a slow kiss. "I know this can't be easy for you."

Jackson rolled his eyes. "Don't go worrying about me. I have your back, Juan. We're dating, remember? Granted you're my first relationship, but I'm pretty sure boyfriends do stuff like this."

Juan grinned. "Boyfriend. Am I just really exhausted or is that word kind of funny? Neither of us are boys, and we're way more than friends."

"I'm not calling you my lover in public," Jackson

said and curled into his side. "Boyfriend will do. Now, how did your talk go?"

Juan rubbed his face against Jackson's silky hair, enjoying his omega's scent. "Good. Really good."

"He said he was proud of me," Lucía said, starting to sob. "I've wanted that for so damn long, and he waited until now to say it."

"Death has a way of changing your perspective," Juan said simply, eyes watering.

"I don't know what Papa's going to do," Lucía said. "Will he want to stay at the house with Dad gone? I live three hours away, and you're in Maine. We can't leave him alone."

"Let's see what he wants," Manuel said, holding her hand. "Let him get through this, then we'll see what he thinks."

Juan didn't want to think past this minute. He didn't want to think about Jorge being gone.

Eventually, Eduardo came out of the room as nurses rushed in. Juan closed his eyes and held back his moan. Jorge Vega was gone.

Juan's papa stood in front of them, shock and despair on his face. "He's gone. I thought… He was stronger today than yesterday. I thought maybe the doctors were wrong. We were talking, then he just closed his eyes and was gone."

Juan and Lucía hugged Eduardo, and Juan let himself go. He cried against the top of his papa's head. He cried for the man he hated and loved, the man he somehow still respected even though he knew he was wrong about so many things. His dad was dead.

❄

THREE DAYS LATER, Juan stood with his family as they lowered his dad's body into the ground. Jackson had an arm around his waist and leaned into him. Juan didn't know what they would have done without Jackson and Manuel.

The two men arranged the funeral and dealt with the insurance people and the lawyer Jorge had filed his will through. They'd taken care of everything so Eduardo, Juan, and Lucía could mourn together.

Behind him stood Carter, Ray, Noah, Ernie, and, of all people, Jimmy. The men had flown out for the funeral and had arrived two days ago. They had been a godsend because his papa was acting strange.

Eduardo insisted he wanted the house sold, so the men and several of Lucía's friends had spent their time packing up the house. Juan didn't know where his papa wanted to go, but he wanted out of the house. Juan had thought he would cling to the memories of Jorge, and there was no better way to do that than in their home.

The pastor finally finished droning on about how good an alpha Juan's dad had been, and the funeral director gestured for them to come forward.

Eduardo tossed a red rose onto the coffin, then walked away. Juan and Jackson followed him, then waited in line to greet and thank each person that had attended the funeral. Juan barely knew what was going on around him, but Jackson prompted him to speak when needed.

Carter hugged him tightly. "Ray and the others

went back to help set up the reception at your house. You need anything, Juan? Please tell us. We love you."

Juan croaked out a laugh and set his forehead against Carter's. "We've had worse, right?"

Carter held his face and pressed his head harder against Juan's. "Family fucks us up. We get it and we're here. I hate I can't do this for you."

They stayed like that for a few moments, then the line moved on. Jackson stayed at his side, arm around his waist, until the end. Juan nodded to the last guest, then turned to his omega.

"Remember last week when you were afraid of committing yourself to an alpha?" he asked.

Jackson snorted, then started laughing, drawing a few disapproving glares. "Remember last week when we were friends with benefits?"

"Those were some good times," Juan said, "but I like this better, blue jay."

"Me too."

CHAPTER 12

JACKSON

Jackson carried out another casserole and set it on the table. "Why does everyone bring a casserole to a reception?" he asked Jimmy.

Jimmy picked up an almost empty tray and arranged a fresh vegetable tray in the center of the table. "I think it's because you can freeze them and eat them later."

"Eduardo doesn't want to stay here," Jackson whispered. "Juan's worried about his papa."

"Can you blame him?" Jimmy said, arching a brow. "Did you see how different the kitchen was from the rest of the house? I get the feeling Jorge was a bit too controlling."

"He was," Jackson said. "Eduardo seemed okay with it though. They loved each other, Jimmy. You and I wouldn't have been able to deal with it, but Juan's papa is different."

"Yeah, you're right." Jimmy shrugged. "How are you

holding up?"

"Me? I'm find. My dad and papa are doing okay."

Jimmy rolled his eyes. "You know what I mean. How are you and Juan doing? This is kinda rough for your first two weeks of dating."

Jackson sighed. "I feel like we've been together for years. We've been friends ever since we met, and I've been in love with him for the past year. Everything just fits, you know? I trust him, Jimmy. I never thought I'd say that about an alpha."

A loud, shrill voice drew his attention. "You're Juan Vega?" A tall, thick woman stood in front of him, arms crossed. Juan stood with Eduardo and Ray in the front room with the family's friends milling around them.

Behind the woman stood a young boy around three years old. A plastic bag full of clothes sat at his feet. He sucked his thumb and clutched a ragged, stuffed llama to his tiny chest. The toddler had big dark eyes and black hair and looked exactly like Juan had at that age. Jackson had seen the damn pictures.

Juan frowned at the woman. "Yes. Can I help you?"

"Yeah, I can't take care of the kid anymore," she said, pointing over her shoulder at the toddler. "I know you said you didn't want him, but I'm getting married, and my man doesn't want me to keep him."

Juan looked baffled. "What the hell are you talking about?"

"Your kid, asshole," the woman said. "You know, the one you had with my brother. Lars is dead, and I've been watching him for months. Can't do it anymore."

Juan flushed. "I've never slept with a guy named Lars. What the hell is going on?"

"I talked on the phone with you when Lars died," she said. "Don't try to lie. Just take the kid, okay?"

Juan looked around her and froze when he saw the kid. Jackson nodded. Juan had seen the pictures too. Juan looked up, meeting his eyes, and Jackson's heart almost broke when he saw the panic in them.

"Holy shit," Jimmy said, grabbing Jackson's arm. "You just fucking said you trusted him. That asshole. You don't just ignore your kid."

"He didn't," Jackson said, voice raw. "He wouldn't."

"Then how do you explain that?" Jimmy asked, looking at him like he was insane. "The kid looks just like that picture you texted me."

Jackson's attention caught on Eduardo's ghost white face. Juan's papa looked ready to faint. "There's an explanation, Jimmy. My alpha's a good man. We'll figure this out."

Lucía pushed through the growing crowd. "Juan, what the hell is wrong with you? You had a kid and just abandoned him?"

Juan seemed frozen in place, eyes focused on Jackson. "Blue jay. This isn't how it looks."

Jackson hurried over. "Of course it isn't. Now, ma'am, do you have custody papers or anything on... Wait, what's his name?" He knelt and met the boy's sad gaze. "What's your name, sweetheart?"

"Oscar," he said, voice almost a whisper.

Jackson smiled at him. "Thank you, Oscar. Will you go with my brother, Jimmy? He'll make you a plate, and you can eat some very yummy food." *Fuck, I hope you like casserole.*

Jimmy smiled and held out his hand. "Hey, little man. I'll feed you."

Oscar took his hand, and they went to the dining room.

Jackson grabbed the plastic bag and stood. "Okay, lady. Papers on Oscar?"

She shrugged. "No. My brother died, and I took him in. Called asshole here, and he told me he didn't want him."

"Juan." Lucía looked so devastated. "How could you?"

"I didn't," Juan said, throwing his hands in the air.

"That doesn't matter now," Jackson said, eyes warning Lucía. "We'll talk about it later. Oscar is with Juan now, and I'll check on if we need to file paperwork or something in the morning." He turned back to the woman. "Thank you. Do you want to leave your number so Oscar can call you?"

She hesitated for a minute. "No. I just had him two months, and he doesn't talk much. There's no point in it. My brother didn't spend much time with him either."

"His name was Lars?" Juan asked.

"Yeah, Lars Miller," she said. "Oscar's birth certificate is in the bag."

"Lars Miller," Juan said, a thoughtful expression on his face. "I went to high school with an omega named Lars Miller."

The woman looked mad again. "Yeah, my brother. The one you fucked and left."

Juan growled. "I didn't –"

"Enough," Ray said, speaking up for the first time. "This isn't the time or place for this. Thank you, ma'am. We have it from here."

She left without another word.

Ray looked at them. "Juan, Lucía, and Jackson. Upstairs. Now."

Lucía frowned. "I don't even know you."

"Come on, Lucía," Jackson hissed.

Ray turned back to Eduardo. "We'll deal with this, okay? Can you stay here, or do you want to be alone?"

Eduardo gave Ray a thankful look. "I'll go to my room. I need to think."

Jackson gave the older omega a hug. "You can meet your grandson tomorrow. Don't worry about anything right now."

Eduardo kissed his cheek. "You are such a good person, Jackson. You have no idea how happy I am that you love my Juan."

Ernie appeared next to Ray and held out his elbow. "Carter and Noah are parting the waves of people. I'll help you escape, Mr. Vega."

Eduardo smiled and took his arm. "Thank you, Ernie. You know, I like you, but I'm glad Juan never got up the courage to ask you out."

Jackson's eyes narrowed on Juan. "Say what?"

Juan groaned and rubbed his eyes. "Can we just start this day over? Please?"

"Upstairs," Ray said, voice hard. "Now."

They ended up in Lucía's old bedroom. Juan's sister paced the floor, tears running down her cheeks. "How could you, Juan? He's just a baby."

"I didn't sleep with Lars Miller," Juan said. He closed his eyes and thought for a moment before opening them again. "I don't even think I was here when Oscar would have been conceived, and I sure as shit didn't get any phone call from that woman."

Jackson winced and shared a look with Ray. "You know, don't you, Dad?"

Ray smiled and hugged him. "No need to *Dad* me right now. I'm not mad at Juan. I know him, and he wouldn't do something like that."

Lucía growled, face reddening. "The kid looks exactly like him."

"Yes," Jackson said. "And exactly like your alpha father."

Juan's jaw went slack, but Lucía just looked confused. "Yeah, that's what I said."

"Lucía," Ray said. "Juan isn't little Oscar's dad. I suspect your father was."

She shook her head, furiously. "No, that's not possible."

"He loved Papa," Juan said, shaking his head too. "No. There has to be another explanation."

"You really didn't do this?" Lucía asked, eyes begging her brother to say he didn't. Jackson seriously felt for her. Over the past few days, it'd been very clear she looked up to Juan.

"No, I didn't," Juan said. He looked at Jackson, eyes watering. "You believe me, don't you?"

Jackson pushed into his arms and pulled his head down for a slow kiss. "I never doubted you for a moment. I *know* you. If Oscar was yours, he'd be living in Maine with you."

"Truth," Ray said, nodding. "We need to figure out if Jorge Vega really is his father or not. I think Eduardo shouldn't have to deal with this, don't you? He's been through too much."

Lucía covered her mouth. "Oh, my god. Did you see the look on his face when he saw Oscar? He knows, doesn't he? If he really thought the boy was Juan's, he would have been pissed and given you the worst lecture of your life."

Jackson hugged Juan tighter. "That was my thought too. He looked like he'd seen a ghost."

"Okay," Ray said, holding his hands up. "I'll do some digging, and we keep Eduardo out of it for now. Let him have some time. Clearly, he doesn't want to deal with this right now."

Jackson jerked away from Juan and dug through the bag still in his hands. He pulled out an envelope and took out the birth certificate. "Oscar Jorge Vega. Father, Juan Vega."

"Why would he put my name on the birth certificate?" Juan asked, shaking his head. "I barely remember him from high school."

"I'll figure things out," Ray said. "Let's go deal with the people downstairs. This is the day you buried your father, and you two deserve time to mourn. Let Jackson and I worry about this right now."

Lucía started crying again and hugged the man. "I still don't know who you are, but I love you."

Jackson grinned widely. "He's my dad."

She leaned back. "What, were you ten when Jackson was born?"

Juan snickered. "Fuck, I love you too, Daddy."

"Damn it, Juan," Ray said, glowering. "When we get back to Hobson Hills, I'm going to bury you in the snow and leave you there."

Lucía sighed. "I'm so confused. I need Manuel." She shook her head as she left.

"We do need to discuss what's going to happen to Oscar," Ray said softly. "He needs someone now."

"He has someone," Jackson said and pulled out his phone. "Juan and I will take care of him. Juan's apartment is way too small, so he'll move in with me. I'll get Yeo to set up the guest room for a little boy. He's just a year or two younger than Linc."

Juan watched him, eyes dark with some emotion. "So, now we're living together?"

"Yes." Jackson nodded slowly. "Follow along, dear. We've progressed from boyfriends to partners."

"Why couldn't we have been partners from the start? I like that word better," Juan said.

"The time wasn't right," Jackson said.

"Yeah, I mean that was this morning," Juan said, laughing. "I do love you, blue jay."

"Good," Ray growled and pulled Juan into a headlock. "You know I will skin you alive if you hurt my son, don't you?"

Jackson ignored them and read the text Jimmy had

sent him. Apparently, Oscar was worn out. Jimmy was putting him to bed in one of the guestrooms.

Jimmy: I'll stay with him tonight while you two figure shit out.

Jackson wasn't sure how he felt about that. He wanted Oscar with him.

He pushed the thought away when Yeo answered the phone. "Jackson? Did the funeral go alright? I know you worried about getting people to carry the casket."

"I need you to set up the guest room as a three-year-old's room, okay? We need pretty much everything, from furniture to clothes to toys. Oh, and don't go into my room."

"It's too late for that," Yeo said. "Min told us about your stuffies. Linc added a few to your collection."

"Damn snitch," Jackson muttered.

"I'm not even going to ask where you picked up a toddler," Yeo said, and Jackson could hear the amusement in his voice. "I'll call Papa, and we'll take care of it."

He hung up the phone and watched Ray give Juan's head a noogie.

This is my alpha, he thought. *I'm in a fucking committed relationship with this man.*

He grinned. He fucking loved it.

CHAPTER 13

JUAN

Juan stared at the little boy sitting on his chest.

Oscar blinked, continuing to suck his thumb.

"Hi," Juan finally said.

"You my daddy?" Oscar asked from around his thumb. "Alex says you my daddy."

It took Juan a minute to translate the baby speak. He supposed Lars's sister's name was Alex. He looked at Jackson. His omega grinned and gave him a thumbs up. *What the fuck does that mean, love of my life?*

Jackson sighed and flicked his ear. "Yes, sweetie. Juan and I are your daddies."

"You is?" Oscar asked and watched Jackson with wide eyes.

"Yes," Jackson said. "I was just telling Juan I wanted his babies, and look, here you are."

"Really?" Oscar turned those big brown eyes on

Juan again. "Daddies takes care the babies. I'm you baby?"

Juan swallowed hard and nodded. It looked like he had a son. Damn, Jackson worked fast. "Yeah. You're my baby."

"I'm big boy," Oscar said, scowling around his thumb. "Not baby."

"I respect that," Juan said, nodding. "You're my big boy."

Oscar looked pleased. "Rays say waff ready."

"Oh, waffles," Jackson said, sitting up. "Thanks, Oscar. We love waffles. You're the best wake-up call in the whole world."

Definitely a wake-up call, Juan thought, wincing when Oscar bounced on him.

"See Dodo?" Oscar held up his ragged llama. "He my llamey."

"I like him," Jackson said and dug under the covers and held up a fuzzy black bear with a knitted cap. "This is Lollipop, my bear."

Oscar bounced again, and Juan moaned. "I likes, I likes!"

"Do you want to hug him?" Jackson asked.

"Yes, peez." Oscar handed Jackson the llama. "You hug Dodo."

"Thank you," Jackson said.

The two hugged their respective stuffies while Juan grinned. He didn't think Jackson realized he would now have to share his stuffed animals with Oscar.

Lucía stood in the doorway, grinning. "Are you three ready for waffles?"

"Uh oh," Oscar said, scooting off Juan. "Yummy, yummy."

The little boy ran out the door, and Lucía smirked at them. "We'll meet you down there."

Jackson set his bear back on the bed and stretched across to lean on Juan. "Are you okay with moving in with me? I know I shouldn't assume things, but really, you practically live there already."

Juan cupped his face. "I've loved you since the day I met you."

Jackson blinked. "Seriously? We met in Tennessee when you all came down to find us for Yeo."

"Yeah," Juan said. "Ray told me about how hard you were working for your family. Then I saw you, and I knew. After that, everything I learned about you only made me more certain."

"Even our Dolly's Diamonds meetings?"

"Those especially," Juan said. "The things you shared with us were so personal. They were integral in understanding who you are. I shared everything I did there because of you."

"Juan." Jackson looked shocked. "For real?"

"Yes." He leaned forward and kissed him. "So, if you're ready for me to move in, I say fuck yeah. I have plans drawn up to renovate your attic into a master bedroom and bath."

"You... Damn it, Juan. I'm going to cry." Jackson sniffed. "Get your ass dressed and let's get waffles before Dad comes and drags us out of here."

"I'm not the naked one," Juan said, standing. He wore his boxers. Jackson had woken him last night during a particularly bad nightmare. They'd found a way to distract Juan and get back to sleep.

Jackson winced. "Is it weird we fucked in your childhood bedroom?"

Juan arched a brow and slid his pants up his legs. "What makes you think this is the first time that's happened?"

Jackson growled. "You were virginal and pure before you met me, Juan. Admit it."

Juan snorted, then ran for the door, trying to button his pants at the same time. He shut the door behind him just in time to miss one of Jackson's UGGs hitting him.

Ray stood at the top of the stairs. He shook his head. "In trouble already, Juan?"

Juan winced when the other shoe hit the door. "We're good, Daddy. Don't worry."

"I hate you," Ray said and went back down the stairs.

A few minutes later, they all sat around the kitchen table. Jackson held Oscar in his lap and glared at Juan from across the table.

Eduardo gave Juan a sad smile. "What did you do, Juan?"

Juan smiled sweetly. "Nothing, Papa. My darling, perfect omega is being mean to me."

Eduardo patted his cheek. "Somehow I don't think that's true. Now, Oscar told me you two are his daddies. Is this true?"

Juan saw the worry in his papa's eyes and wondered

if Lucía was right. Maybe Papa did know something. "Yep. He's my son, alright. Jackson and me want kids, and now, we have our first."

"You've just been dating for a couple of weeks," Lucía said. "Jackson, are you sure about this?"

"We've technically been dating for only a few days," Jackson said. "Juan's been pining after me for years though, so we're basically married now. I even took his virginity. It's just like Elizabeth Bennett and Mr. Darcy. I, of course, being the brooding and handsome Mr. Darcy." They all stared at Jackson, but Juan's omega just shrugged. "What?"

"Juan *is* feisty, smart, and independent," Jimmy said, thoughtfully.

"Anyway," Juan said, interrupting their laughter. "I'm on Oscar's birth certificate, so I don't think there will be any problem taking him home when we go. Yeo, Jackson's brother, is setting up a room for him."

"We'll start on the attic renovations when we get home," Carter said, munching on a piece of bacon. "Tomás is handling things well back home because jobs have slowed down a bit. We'll have the time. I'll have him start getting materials."

"If you're moving in with Jackson, then I'll take over the lease for your apartment," Eduardo said.

Lucía gasped. "Papa, you're moving away?"

Eduardo sighed. "I need some time away, Lucía. I'll be back to help with the wedding."

Manuel wrapped an arm around Lucía. "I'll take care of selling the house if you want, Eduardo."

"Thank you, Manuel. You and Jackson have been such a big help," Eduardo said, smiling. He looked around the table. "You all have. Thank you for all the work you've done the last few days."

"Not a problem," Carter said, signing the conversation to Noah. "We kinda like Juan, so we're happy to help."

"It doesn't seem real," Lucía said.

Eduardo sniffed and wiped his eyes. "No, it doesn't. Last week, he seemed okay. He was more tired than usual, but of course he wouldn't talk about that. I don't know what to do. I just know I don't want to stay here."

"Your world has been rocked," Ray said. "Give it time, and it'll settle again. It will never be the same, but it's still yours."

Lucía smiled. "Thanks, Ray."

Juan ate his waffles and watched Carter and Ernie distract Eduardo with pictures of their kids. Ray spoke quietly with Lucía and Manuel about the house, and Noah and Jimmy were currently trying to see who could eat a waffle faster. The winner was Jimmy.

His omega helped Oscar eat his breakfast, a look of contentment on his face. Jackson loved playing with all the Wilson littles and his own younger brothers. Juan guessed he really had meant it when he said he wanted his own kids.

His dad would have been upset that they were all so loud. He had been a firm believer of eating in silence when you were at the table. Juan closed his eyes. He didn't want to think about his dad.

They had to be wrong about him. He had adored Eduardo. He had lectured, over and over, about finding an omega to take care of and honor. He couldn't have cheated on Juan's papa.

An hour later, he found Ray packing up the upstairs hall bathroom.

Ray looked at him. "You want me to tell you if it was your dad or not."

Juan nodded. "I don't want it to be him. As much as we butted heads, I never doubted he loved my papa. I can't believe he would do that. I can't."

Ray taped the last box closed. "The man just died, and your emotions are all over the place. You may not like the answers I find, Juan."

"Maybe not, but they'll be answers and not speculation."

"I'll call you when I find something." Ray handed him two of the boxes. "By the way, I can't stand that you and Jackson are together. It makes me feel old."

Juan rolled his eyes. "Jackson's not your biological son. How does this make you feel old?"

"I practically raised him," Ray said and pushed Juan out the door. "Now, my best friend is his Elizabeth Bennett. It's just wrong."

"Practically raised him? He was twentyish when you met him," Juan yelled as Ray walked away.

"Daddy," Oscar said from behind him, making Juan jump.

"Hey, buddy. Whatcha need?"

"I has to potty." Oscar danced in place. "Potty is tall."

Juan set the boxes down and hurried back into the bathroom. He didn't want to start fatherhood with a potty accident. He'd rather save all those for Carter and his kids.

132

Jackson was so happy to be home. Yeo and Papa had picked them all up from the airport, then Papa had taken Eduardo to his new apartment to settle in. Mrs. Odell had promised to keep an eye on the older omega.

Jackson set his suitcase on the floor, then dropped to his knees. "Miss Mona, my pretty little girl." He hugged his wiggling dog. She wore her unicorn horn this morning.

Ines and Min-Jun watched him from the couch. A very fluffy brown puppy sat on Jackson's grandpapa. The puppy watched him, tongue hanging out.

"You must be Bigfoot," Jackson said.

The puppy hopped off Min-Jun, making him grunt, then ran to Jackson, wiggling in beside Miss Mona to lick Jackson's face.

The Christmas tree shook as Onyx crashed through the branches until he reached the floor. Jackson's cat ran for him and launched himself into his human's arms as soon as he was close.

"How are my precious babies? Did you miss me?" Jackson kissed his cat's head and listened to his rumbling purr. "You have a new brother. Don't look at me like that Miss Mona, I know you just met Bigfoot. You'll like Oscar. I promise."

"Blue jay, you gonna just keep blocking the door?" Juan asked from behind him, Oscar riding on his back.

The little boy looked over Juan's shoulder, then gasped. "Puppy. Kitty."

Jackson scooted forward so Juan could set Oscar down. The little boy sat between Miss Mona and Bigfoot and giggled as the dogs licked his face. Onyx watched, uncertain of the toddler.

"Kitty?" Oscar held his hand out, and Onyx butted it with his hand, deeming the mini human worthy of his time.

"I'm glad you all made it home," Min-Jun said. "You must be Oscar."

"Hi," Oscar said, waving.

Min-Jun smiled. "I'm your greatpapa."

"Greatpapa," Oscar repeated, face scrunched in concentration. "Me has grandpapa too!"

"He met Papa at the airport," Jackson said, smiling.

Oscar looked at Ines in expectation. "Who you?"

She laughed. "I'm your bisabuela. You'll love me the most, pequeño, I just know it."

Min-Jun took Oscar's hand. "We'll show you around your new home, sweetie. Miss Mona and Bigfoot will help us."

Jackson grinned as he watched them walk around the house. He looked up at Juan. "I'm so happy to be home."

Juan smiled and pulled him up. "Me too. I'll get the bags upstairs." He nodded toward the Christmas tree. "I think there are more presents there than when we left."

Jackson went and looked at the name tags. "Looks like Oscar was a good boy this year."

"We have some good families, don't we?" Juan asked him as they made their way upstairs. "Christmas is just two days away, and there's no way we could have done all this ourselves."

"They're alright," Jackson said, tearing up when he saw Oscar's room. "Damn, they went all out."

The small room had even been repainted a soft baby blue. Harper had obviously donated the furniture from his stockpile of premade pieces. A toddler bed with a thick, white knitted blanket sat in one corner, and a dresser and toybox took up another wall. The small bookshelf next to the door was even already full of children's books.

"Okay, they may be more than just alright," Jackson said. He wanted to take his boots off and sink his toes in that huge furry rug. Where did that even come from?

Juan moved behind him and nibbled Jackson's neck. "Min-Jin and Ines have our boy. You want to make sure our bed still works?"

Jackson wiggled, dick already hardening. "It's the responsible thing to do."

"No one wants a broken bed," Juan agreed, and they ran to the bedroom, flinging the door open.

"Uh," Jackson said, blinking as he looked around the room. There were kids everywhere, and they were playing with his stuffed animals.

"Hey, Uncle Jay," Linc said, waving. Him and his best friend, Iggy, were leaning against one of Jackson's stuffed penguins with a book spread across their laps. Linc's pet rabbit, Huckleberry, sat between the boys.

Nari, Jackson's niece, was laying down beside her best friend, Nate. They were telling stories to the stuffed bears and rabbits surrounding them.

David and Sawyer's twins were in a pile of Jackson's remaining stuffed animals with Carter's twins who just happened to be *their* best friends. All four were passed out, sleeping. Obviously, they had been playing hard for a little too long.

Min came running from where he had been bouncing with Bea on Jackson's other penguin. "Jay Jay! Miss you."

Jackson caught his little brother up and hugged him tightly. "Did you bring all your friends to play with my stuffies?"

"Uh huh," Min said, nodding. "We share. Look!" He held out a soft stuffed raccoon. "For you."

Jackson grinned and kissed his brother's cheek. "You're the best little brother ever, Mini-Boo."

Someone tugged at the bottom of his coat. He looked down and found Harper's oldest boy, Rue. The little boy had just turned three right before Juan and

Jackson had started dating. He was a cute kid, with chocolate colored skin and dark eyes.

"Mr. Jay, Daddy told me that you was giving me a best friend for Christmas. Are they here yet?" Rue asked, eyes hopeful.

Jackson shared a confused look with Juan. "Um, I don't know, Rue."

Min-Jun and Oscar pushed in behind them. "Here's your daddies' room, Oscar, and this is the little boy I told you about. His name is Rue."

Oscar smiled shyly and waved. "Hi. We best friends?"

Rue's grin stretched across his face. "Yeah. Let's play."

Oscar giggled and followed Rue to a pile of building blocks in front of the window.

Jackson's eyes watered. "I think that may have been the sweetest thing I ever saw."

Juan nodded, smiling softly. "Did Harper really tell Rue we were bringing him a best friend?"

Min-Jun grinned. "Yes. All the other Wilson littles have their special friends, but Rue was just a little too young for Linc and Iggy, and a little too old for Carter and David's sets of twins. He'll help Oscar settle in, and now, he can have his own person."

Jackson hugged his grandpapa, squishing Min between them. "I don't know how I feel about you sharing my collection with a bunch of babies."

Min-Jun rolled his eyes. "Don't look at me. Min brought them all here. They were playing downstairs, and Min led them straight to your collection." He patted Jackson's cheek. "I don't understand why you hid all those cute stuffies away, baby boy, but I'm glad you aren't keeping them secret anymore."

Jackson mock-glared at Min and pretended to eat his belly. "No secrets with this snitch."

"We'll wrangle them all up and bring them back to my house," Ines said, chuckling. "Rue is staying here until Grey and Harper finish their Christmas shopping. I can't tear apart best friends."

Jackson watched Oscar and Rue talk quietly, heads pressed together. Miss Mona sat on one side of them and Bigfoot on the other. "I'm okay with that."

It took some doing, but Ines and Min-Jun gathered all the kids and herded them back next door.

Linc handed Jackson a stuffed Christmas gnome on the way out. "For your collection, Uncle Jay. I'll bring more later. 'Kay?"

Jackson sighed and hugged his nephew. "You're the best, Linc. I'll see you tomorrow."

Soon enough, they were gone, and Oscar and Rue had moved to Oscar's room to play.

Jackson looked at Juan. "We can't fuck, can we?"

Juan gave him a sad look. "Afternoon nookie will have to wait. Oscar's probably hungry, and he'll need a nap soon to deal with the time change."

They heard the buzz of a skill saw and looked up. "Is someone in the attic?" Jackson asked.

Juan snorted. "Surely Tomás didn't already start the renovation."

They went to the narrow attic stairway and climbed it single file, Juan in the front. Jackson clutched the back of his alpha's sweater and peeked over his shoulder.

Tomás and several others were walking around the large attic. It looked like a master bathroom and large walk-in closet had already been framed. Gramps and his youngest son, Marco, were hanging the sheetrock around the bare frames. Tomás and Luke were stuffing insulation into the hollow crevices of the unfinished walls of the large space.

Shawn, one of Marco's sons, grinned and waved at them. "Hey, you two. Hope we weren't making too much noise."

Juan shook his head. "What are you guys doing?"

Gramps came and hugged Juan. "I'm so sorry about your dad, Juan. Carter sent us those plans you made for the attic, and we wanted to do something for you. We couldn't be there for you at your dad's funeral, but we could start working on your renovation."

"Luke and I did the floor yesterday," Tomás said, stomping a foot on the refinished hardwood. "This is some tough stuff. I didn't think it would look so good, but damn was I wrong."

"Luke?" Jackson asked, looking amazed. "I didn't know you could manual labor so well."

Luke groaned and rolled his shoulders. "It was horrible. They made me get on my hands and knees, Jay, and I couldn't even wear my favorite tie."

Shawn laughed and slapped the alpha's shoulder. "You'll be back to selling things soon enough, pretty boy."

Jackson looked surprised. "Your parents rehired you?"

Luke's face grew dark. "No. I'm done with them. They won't accept that I'm having a baby with Griff, so fuck them."

"He'll be selling cars for me," Shawn said. "George and I having been buying up pieces of junk and fixing them up. We have twelve ready to go now. Luke here purchased the lot next to my garage, and he'll be selling them."

"I know how to run a dealership, and I'll get plenty of business from the surrounding towns," Luke said, eyes determined.

Jackson hugged him. "I'm so proud of you."

Tomás waved them toward the door. "Go rest or something. We'll talk with you before painting the walls. When Harper gets here, send him up. I want to ask him about some shelves."

Juan gave him a suspicious look. "How do you know Harper's stopping here?"

"Rue and Oscar are best friends," Tomás said, rolling his eyes. "Grey and Harper decided that's how it was going to be."

"Speaking of Oscar," Gramps said, wiping his hands on his pants. "I'm gonna go say hi to the little tyke. We've been looking forward to another great-grandbaby."

Juan tilted his head. "He's not technically your –"

Jackson elbowed him. "Gramps is *my* grandpa. You know that, Juan. Hush and let him go see Oscar."

Juan grinned. "Okay, okay."

Jackson pulled him back downstairs and into their room. "Holy shit, our friends move fast."

"We do the same for them," Juan said, shrugging. "I don't even know why I'm surprised."

Jackson heard Juan's phone buzz, and his alpha looked at the screen before answering it. "Hey, Papa. Are you doing alright?" He listened for a minute, then started laughing. "She's not crazy. You can let her in. Love you too." He hung up.

Jackson pushed Juan on the bed, then sat in his lap. Onyx hopped up beside them, then crawled onto Jackson. "What happened?"

"Papa was starting to unpack. Dean and Susan were helping him, then Fawn showed up."

"What did she want?" Jackson asked. Fawn was an odd woman. She was extremely wealthy but was still emotionally recovering from her previous marriage. It had been very rough. She was also struggling to rebuild her relationship with her estranged daughter, Summer.

That was why Fawn had moved to Hobson Hills. She tried, but she stuck out in a town of blue-collar workers and laid back, family-oriented people.

"Basically, Fawn did exactly what Rue did," Juan said, shaking his head. "She arrived and told Papa he was going to be her friend. She said everyone else had a best friend, and he was going to be hers."

"Did they play with blocks and cuddle?" Jackson asked, laughing.

"More along the lines of she's helping him unpack." Juan sighed. "I'm kinda glad for both of them. I think

Fawn needs someone to talk to, and Papa never had a lot of friends."

Jackson kissed Juan. "I think things will be okay. We just need some time to settle."

"Yes," Juan said, then kissed him again. "We probably have fifteen minutes before someone else arrives."

Jackson smiled. "I know exactly how to use it."

Juan smirked. "How do you want me?"

"On your back," Jackson said and pushed Juan. When his alpha lay flat, Jackson lay across him and propped his chin on his fist. "How are you doing? Really."

Juan pouted. "No sex?"

"Just feelings," Jackson said.

"The dreams have been bad," Juan said. "It's all mixed up in my head. I see my friends die, but then Dad is there too. He wasn't really there, but in my head, he's lying in pieces beside Dylan and Julio."

"I think that's understandable," Jackson said. "Him dying was a shock. It's bound to haunt you for a while."

Juan rubbed his face. "I think I need a Dolly's Diamonds and Dragons session."

"I'll call them now," Jackson said.

CHAPTER 15

Jackson hugged Grey one more time. "Thank you so much for this."

Grey rolled his eyes and patted his son Auggie's back. "It's no problem. I get to watch the cuteness of Rue and Oscar together, so this is hardly a chore."

Jackson had arranged an emergency meeting of Dolly's Diamonds and Dragons, and, fortunately, Gray and Harper had agreed to watch Oscar while they went.

"Thank you for all the books too," Jackson said. "Don't think I didn't notice all your gifts."

Grey blushed. "They'll all be for sale at The Book Worm soon. You just get my homemade copies."

"They're perfect," he said.

"We'll have dinner waiting for you when you get back," Harper said, grinning as he spun around the living room with a giggling boy over each shoulder. "I need to talk to Shawn about those shelves anyway."

Grey nudged Juan with his shoulder. "Go. Get out. Leave me with the cuteness."

Juan grinned. "We'll be back soon."

They left and drove the short distance to the library. It was too damn cold to walk this late in the afternoon.

The room was already set up when they went in, and everyone was gathered in a circle. Valentina met them at the door, hugging them both. "I made cake for you."

Abel waved, mouth covered in frosting. "It's edible too." He shoved another bite into his mouth.

Jackson pulled Juan to a chair and sat him down. "Thank you all for meeting at the last minute. We have a bit of an emergency."

"Are you pregnant?" Mrs. Odell said, eyes brightening. "We've noticed you two finally stopped dancing around each other with those stupid looks of longing."

"I thought it was romantic," Ms. Byrd said, wrinkling her nose. "You two certainly took long enough though."

"No," Jackson said, rolling his eyes. "I'm not pregnant, but we do have a kid."

"We heard," Drew said, snickering. "It's all over town."

"You guys should come meet Oscar soon," Juan said, trying to smile. "Our emergency has a bit to do with that."

"Tell us what you can, sweetheart," Mrs. Odell said, reaching over to pat his hand.

Jackson got a large piece of the cake, sitting on the table and ate it while Juan told them all about his father dying and the mystery of Oscar.

"You're sure he can't be yours?" Abel asked. "Ernie told me he looks just like you."

"No," Juan said. "I did the numbers, and I wasn't even in the state when he was conceived. I was on a beach in Florida. That was before I moved here to work with Carter."

"How do you feel about all this?" Drew asked. "About your dad?"

Juan squeezed his eyes shut. "I'm so fucking mad at him. He hid that he had cancer and refused treatment. The doctors told us that chemo and surgery would have given him a really good chance of survival. He didn't want to lose his hair and look weak in front of his friends."

Jackson wrapped an arm around Juan's shoulders. He couldn't stand the pain in his alpha's voice.

"He chose to die and leave Papa and us with this mess. He *chose* it," Juan said, practically growling. "I am so damn mad at him."

Valentina sniffled and came to sit on Juan's other side. "You miss him too though. Don't you?"

A small moan escaped Juan, and he hugged Valentina tightly, tears falling fast. "Yes, damn it. All I've ever wanted from him is love and respect. I looked up to the bastard, even with his old-fashioned views and stubbornness. I love him, and I don't want him to be gone."

Valentina sobbed against Juan's shoulder, and

Jackson cried as he stroked Juan's back, letting his alpha mourn.

"It sucks feeling this way," Valentina said. "But you guys told me that it's okay to be sad and angry and any other feeling. You're allowed to get mad at him, Juan. He shouldn't have left you. He shouldn't have been selfish. It's okay to miss him too. He was your dad. You loved him."

Ms. Byrd wiped her eyes. "The day we discover our parents are human beings with flaws and ugliness is one of the worst. I think we hold on to the idea that they're somehow superhuman and will always be there or will always make the right choice."

"They don't," Mrs. Odell said. "He chose what he wanted instead of what his family needed, and even after going on about how an alpha's duty is take care of his family."

Abel huffed and pushed himself out of his seat. "This calls for some Dolly." He dug through their records and put one on.

The familiar notes of "If I had Wings" started to play, and Jackson pressed his face against Juan's back as they sang and swayed to the song. He let himself get lost in the emotions filling the room. His poor alpha hurt so much.

The last notes of the song died away and silence filled the room.

Juan looked up from where his face had been buried against Valentina's hair. "I don't want to be like him. Jackson doesn't trust easily, and I don't want to hurt him like my dad hurt Papa."

Jackson couldn't help it – he started laughing. Juan turned around, staring at him in shock. Then Mrs. Odell started chuckling, and before they knew it, everyone but Juan was laughing.

Jackson leaned over and bit Juan's shoulder through his thick jacket. "My beautiful, idiotic alpha. You aren't a thing like your father."

"I want a family like him," Juan argued. "I work construction, look like him, and I want to take care of you and make you happy."

"Yeah," Jackson said, nodding, "but would you try to *tame* me and train me to be the exact way you think an omega should act? Hell, do you even think omegas should act a certain way?"

Juan shook his head. "No. You're my blue jay, and omegas are just people. You have annoyingly handsome omegas who collect stuffed animals and quirky omegas that like to knit."

"Don't forget the ones that love Dolly Parton and brewing beer," Abel said, grinning.

"I just… I respected him," Juan said. "I thought he was a hardass but a man who put his family first. What if I do start thinking like him? I still hear his voice in my head telling me to man up and quit crying."

"If you start acting like he did, then Jackson will take care of it," Drew said, smiling. "You're not alone, Juan. If you have some stupid idea in your head, you know we'll let you know you're acting like an idiot."

"Like the idea that you'd do the same stuff your dad did," Jackson said, leaning over and biting Juan again. "Bad Juan!"

"You're the one biting me," Juan said, scowling. "At least I can behave in public."

Valentina snorted, then covered her nose. "Oops. I was just remembering how we saw you climb under a table to avoid Ray."

Ms. Byrd chuckled. "I think it's time for another Dolly song." She stood and put another record on. The lyrics for "Light of a Clear Blue Morning" filled the room.

Valentina stood and pulled Juan up as she sang along. Juan laughed, eyes still full of tears. The two sang and danced around the chairs. Drew and Mrs. Odell followed their example, and Ms. Byrd swayed next to the record player.

Jackson laughed and sang as he got another piece of cake. He was so damn hungry lately. He sat beside Abel and bumped his shoulder against him. The omega grinned at him, and they hit a high note together.

When the song was over, they sat back down, and Jackson noticed Juan looked a lot better.

Mrs. Odell stood. "Now, what would Rashona from *The Dragon of the Green Wood* say?"

Jackson pinched Juan's side. "She'd say we choose the kind of person we are. The only way someone can control you is if you let them."

"She reminds me of a young Dolly," Mrs. Odell said, nodding. "Now, Juan, you are a good person, and your omega loves you. Have more faith in yourself."

Valentina handed him a piece of cake. "Have some cake."

By the time they got home from the meeting, they

were both emotionally exhausted.

Juan parked under the carport. "That was just what I needed, blue jay."

Jackson took his hand. "Me too. I think I ate three pieces of cake."

"You ate four." Juan smirked.

"A kind and loving partner would say I only ate one piece," Jackson said, eyes narrowed.

"That's what I meant to say." Juan gave him an innocent look. "You only ate one tiny piece, my beloved partner."

"Better," Jackson said and got out of the car. "Is it me or are there even more cars here than when we left?"

Eduardo met them at the door, holding Onyx. "Juan, this woman keeps following me around."

Fawn stood behind them, looking like a magazine-perfect snow bunny. "Hi, boys. Everyone just kind of showed up and started cooking. I think there are over twenty people here."

"Hey, Fawn," Jackson said. "How's it going?"

"Very well," she said, arm on Eduardo's shoulder. "Eduardo here is going bowling with me tomorrow night. Doesn't that sound fun? I've never been bowling before."

"That does sound fun," Juan said, smiling at his papa. "Are you really upset she's following you around? I know how to distract her."

Eduardo sighed. "No. She's fine. She just makes me talk about Jorge. It's good and bad."

"Just like me," Fawn said, grinning. "Do you want to

put more ornaments over their fireplace?"

"Yes," Eduardo said, pouting. "I ran out of room at the apartment."

"His place looks like the north pole," Fawn said, shaking her head. "It makes him happy, I suppose."

Jackson pulled the woman into a hug. "I love you, Fawn."

"Oh, dear. I love you too, darling. Now let me go." She patted his head.

He laughed, then followed Juan through the packed kitchen. There was a lot of food spread out on the counters, so he started loading up a plate.

"You're hungry?" Juan asked, brows raised.

"Don't act surprised," Jackson said. "I'm a growing boy."

Oscar ran into the room. "Daddies! Santa bring presents. You see?"

"We saw all those presents for you under the tree," Juan said, kneeling to hug the little boy. "You were good this year, huh?"

"Alex say me not good," Oscar said. "No presents ever."

Jackson frowned. He didn't like Oscar being told he wasn't good. "Ignore anything Alex told you. You're a very good boy, Oscar. We're your daddies, so we know."

He clapped and kissed Juan's cheek. "Go play Rue now." He turned and ran away.

Juan gave him a sad look. "Jackson, I don't care who his real bio father is. He's our son, right?"

"Yes," Jackson said, nodding. "He's our son."

CHAPTER 16

JUAN - CHRISTMAS DAY

*J*uan peeked into Oscar's room. His son was curled into a little ball on his bed and surrounded by stuffed animals. Dodo still took prominence in Oscar's arms, but there were several new favorites.

It had snowed another couple of feet last night, and the morning was going to be cold, but it was Christmas. Juan couldn't wait for Oscar to get up so they could open presents. Christmas with a kid was so much better than Christmas by himself.

Jackson slapped his back. "Let him sleep. We can finish making breakfast before he gets up."

"What kid sleeps late on Christmas day?"

"One who's never had a Christmas," Jackson said. "He's just three, and who knows how it was for him last year."

Juan sighed. "Yeah. Ugh, I hate this."

Eduardo stood at the top of the stairs with the dogs. "Is he awake yet?"

Jackson laughed. "You two are worse than kids."

Oscar's door opened, and the little boy looked up at them. "Presents time?"

Juan grinned and picked him up, tossing him in the air. "Yes!"

"Bathroom first," Jackson said sternly. "Then presents. Then breakfast."

"Potty now," Oscar said, giggling. "Want presents."

"Yes, sir," Juan said and ran down the hall with Oscar.

A few minutes later, Juan watched his son open present after present. *Maybe we went a little overboard.*

"Stuffie." Oscar giggled and hugged the big white polar bear. "Loves."

Nope. He gets everything he wants from now until eternity.

Jackson leaned against his shoulder. "This is the best Christmas ever."

Miss Mona walked past them with her new mistletoe headband. Onyx was perched at the top of the tree again, and Bigfoot snuggled next to Eduardo.

Juan kissed his head. "Yeah. It is. Thank you, Jackson. For giving this to me." He threaded their fingers together.

"You give me too much credit, but I'll take it," Jackson said. "It beats what I got you for Christmas."

Juan laughed and held up the Dolly Parton coffee mug. "I don't think you could have picked something better."

Eduardo held up his own knitted sweater. "This is

beautiful and handy. I didn't expect it to be so cold here."

"Definitely colder than Arizona," Jackson agreed. "Wait until you see the rest of your gifts."

Juan pursed his lips. Ernie *may* have gone a bit overboard with gifts for both Eduardo and Oscar.

"Lucía said she was coming up here next year," Eduardo said. "You'd think she had never seen snow. She loved the pictures I sent her."

"Hat," Oscar said, pulling out a knitted hate with bear ears and sticking it on his head. "Me bear. Grr."

Juan snorted. "I love it, Oscar." He leaned into Jackson. "How many more presents does he have. I'm starting to get hungry."

"Six more," Jackson said. "Then we eat and go to Papa's house for more presents."

"I think I'll bake some cookies, then nap," Eduardo said, yawning.

"Um, no," Jackson said. "You're going with us. Fawn will be there too. You can bake cookies together."

Eduardo brightened. "Do you know how much fun bowling is?"

Juan hid his smile. His papa had called him after he went bowling and spent an hour telling him how much fun it was. Fawn was an odd choice for a friend for Eduardo, but who was he to judge?

An hour later, they were opening more presents. Min helped Oscar with his, the two boys sitting close together. Eduardo and Fawn sat together on the loveseat and oohed and ahhed over each other's gifts.

Jake and Jules ran around the room, playing Santa's

helpers. "Here, Juan." Jules handed Juan a box, then hugged him. "Love you." Then he was off to grab another present under the tree.

Juan looked at the tag, and his eyes widened. "From Daddy?" He looked at Ray. "Seriously?"

Ray groaned. "Dean wrapped the presents, okay?"

Dean grinned. "It is what it is, hero."

Juan laughed and unwrapped his gift. "Holy shit, it's the newest infrared goggles. How did you know?"

"You force me to go on those stupid excursions, and you complain about your goggles every time," Ray said, shrugging. "It wasn't exactly hard."

"You're the best daddy ever," Juan said, hugging the goggles to his chest.

"I'm a little disturbed," Jimmy said, shaking his head.

"You aren't the only one," Yeo said, opening his own gift.

Jackson held a wide, flat box to his ear and shook it. "What did you get me, Yeo?"

Yeo watched him, excitement in his eyes. "Open it and see."

Jackson tore the paper off and opened the box. When he frowned, Juan looked over his shoulder. There was a stack of papers inside. They looked important.

Jackson shuffled through them, eyes widening. "Yeo, you can't be serious."

Yeo shrugged. "You do half the work already. You deserve to share in half the profits."

Juan grinned. "Is that what I think it is?"

Yeo nodded. "I want Jackson to be my partner at The Book Worm. It's already *our* store. I just want it to be official." His eyes softened when he watched Caden help their daughter unwrap a present. "You have a family now, Jackson, and I know how important it is to put down roots. Be my partner. Please?"

Jackson swallowed. "Are you sure?"

Juan rubbed his back, knowing Jackson still didn't realize how smart and helpful he really was.

"Absolutely." Yeo nodded without any hesitancy.

"Okay." Jackson laughed nervously. "Shit. What a Christmas gift. I only got you some manties."

Caden pumped his fist in the air. "Thank you, Jackson."

Jake rushed by and handed Jackson another gift to open while Jules brought one for Yeo. Jackson still looked dazed from Yeo's gift, and Juan wanted to dance him across the room. He looked around. *It's too crowded for that, damn it.*

He whispered against Jackson's ear. "I'm proud of you, blue jay. You and your brother make a good team."

Jackson pulled his head down for a kiss. "We're going to have a good life, Juan. Aren't we?"

"Hell yeah."

Min barreled into him. "No. Bad word."

Dean snickered. "You keep an eye on him, Min."

They finished opening presents, then ate lunch. The younger kids took their naps, then it was off to Gramps and Grammy's house for Christmas dinner.

Grammy hugged him as soon as he walked in the door. "We're so glad you came. Just so you know, I'm stealing your papa for the quilting club. Clarice said we need a new member so she'll no longer be the newbie. Ines is also making him join the baking club. He's such a sweet man."

"Thanks, Grammy," he whispered in her ear. "I'm worried about him."

She leaned back and gave him a hard look. "That man is stronger than you think."

Jackson set Oscar down, and the little boy ran off to find Rue. Juan wrapped an arm around his blue jay. "I didn't think I could eat again, but damn, look at that."

Grammy and several others had cooked quite a dinner. There was turkey, ham, roast, and what seemed like a million side dishes and desserts.

Jackson pushed him away. "Out of my way. I'm starving."

Juan watched him go, then looked at Grammy. "Do you think he might be..."

She grinned, eyes twinkling. "You never know, Juan. Yeo told me the first month or two of his pregnancies, he was always hungry."

"He threw up this morning too." Juan rubbed his chin. "We better finish the renovation soon."

She laughed and patted his shoulder. "You'll figure it out."

Noah waved at him from a corner, and he went to his friend. Sometimes, Juan thought being around Noah was like a calm in the storm. The young alpha didn't seem to let anything bother him too much.

"Will you do me a favor?" Noah asked, voice a little too loud.

"Sure," Juan said. "What do you need?"

Noah leaned forward, and his voice lowered a bit. "Justin is trying to set me up with Griff. I like Griff, but we're just friends."

Juan eyed him and signed as he spoke. "Why not give Griff a chance?"

Noah sighed, then looked away. "I'm kind of involved with someone. I think anyway."

Juan smacked his arm. "Who? Why didn't you tell me?"

"I haven't told anyone. It's too new." Noah blushed. "It's not a big deal."

"You haven't dated anyone since, you know." Juan waved around his ears. Noah had joined the army and been deployed quickly. Unfortunately, the very first day of his deployment, he had been in an ambush that resulted in his loss of hearing.

"Everyone is settling down," Noah said, shrugging. "I wanted to but hadn't met anyone until now."

"I'll distract Justin," Juan said, wondering if Justin even knew about Griff being pregnant. He looked around. *Oh yeah, Justin knows.*

Griff's brothers sat on each side of him. Justin was trying to force feed Griff a plate of food, and Zed was glaring at Luke, his eyes threatening imminent death.

"It may not be too hard to do," Juan said, patting Noah's shoulder.

The rest of the evening was a loud, raucous mess of food, laughter, and presents. Juan needed a little peace, so he hid in the kitchen with Ernie's husband, Reuben. The other alpha had social anxiety, so he often spent his time in the kitchen during family gatherings. Tonight, he was joined by Juan and Bennett. They sat at the table and watched Reuben work.

The large man cut potatoes and put them on to boil. He looked at Juan over his shoulder. "Remember Thanksgiving?"

Juan leaned back and closed his eyes, smiling. "It was definitely worth the risk." Reuben had encouraged him to take a chance with Jackson. *Fuck, it feels like a century ago.*

Bennett took a bite of a Christmas cookie. "It's Christmas evening, Juan. Did Santa grant your Christmas wish?"

Juan thought back to just a few weeks ago. *I wished that Jackson loved me like I love him. I wished he was my omega.* He thought about Jackson's acceptance of him, then his trust. He hadn't doubted Juan when he'd told him he hadn't just abandoned Oscar. He loved Juan and he trusted him.

"Yeah. I got my Christmas wish," he said softly. *I got my family.*

CHAPTER 17

JUAN - FEBRUARY

Juan finished showering and quickly brushed his teeth. He had two small jobs to complete today, then had to stop by and cuddle Abel's newborn, Emma. Abel's friend had given birth a few weeks ago, and Emma was a cute little bald angel with a healthy pair of lungs.

After that, Jackson and he were taking Oscar to watch a movie. It would be the little boy's first movie, and he was excited about bubble critters or something like that. Juan was excited about cuddling with Jackson in a dark theater.

He left the bathroom and noticed Jackson was still sleeping, Onyx curled up next to his head. His omega cuddled a soft, stuffed raccoon. Jackson had seemed more tired than usual the last few weeks. Right after Christmas, he had taken the pregnancy test. They would be welcoming a little one into the world sometime in September.

Juan went to the closet and dug out his clothes.

Their renovated room had a lot of space for them. It even held about half of Jackson's books and all of his stuffed animals. The rest of his books and plants still dominated the living room, and Juan loved it. Jackson was a pack rat, and he was okay with that.

The large rose window above the bed was frosted over. It was damn cold outside. *I wish I could just crawl back into bed.*

He leaned over Jackson and kissed his head. It was too early for him to get up for work. Miss Mona looked up from where she slept at the foot of the bed. Juan took a minute to brush her bangs and pick a headband for her. He booped her nose, then left, quietly shutting the door behind him.

He went down the attic stairs and noticed Oscar's door was open, and Bigfoot lay across the threshold. In just a few weeks, their puppy had sprouted. He was about twice the size he'd been and was still growing. He was also very protective of his humans.

Juan stepped over the dog and checked on his son. Oscar wasn't in his bed, so Juan looked around and spotted him curled on one of Jackson's giant penguins. Juan grinned and leaned down to kiss Oscar's head. *You take after your blue jay daddy.*

Juan knew better than to make coffee that Jackson couldn't drink, so he stopped by Zoe's bakery to grab a cup.

She handed him his cup along with a bagel. "Here you go, handsome."

Juan winked. "I'll also go ahead and pay for

Jackson's morning mint tea. He'll be by in a couple of hours."

"Sure thing. You still good for our renovation next week?" Zoe asked.

Juan nodded. He was expanding the master bath in Zoe and Gib's apartment. He was getting back in his truck when his phone rang. *Ray.* "Hey."

"I found out who Oscar's father is," Ray said bluntly.

Juan swallowed. "I'll be at your place in a few minutes."

"Alright."

Juan ended the call and texted Carter. His friend would rearrange their schedule or get Tomás to cover the jobs today.

He sat in the truck for a few minutes. *Do I want to know?*

He started the engine, then backed out of his parking spot. *I have to know.*

Ray met Juan on the porch of his large cabin. He had Jun on his hip, and Min danced in place beside him. Ray's expression didn't look too promising. "Come inside."

"Dean's not here?" Juan followed him into the house, dread filling him with every step he took.

"My cowboy has early days." Ray handed Jun to Jimmy and tickled Min before sending him to play with Jules. He led Juan to the kitchen and sat him down at the table before turning his laptop to face Ray.

On the screen was a picture of Juan's dad kissing a vaguely familiar omega. Juan remembered Lars Miller as a tiny blond teenager with a bit of a wild side. He'd never spent a lot of time with him, but it was more that they didn't run in the same circles.

"So it *was* him." All the grief and anger that he had dealt with the past couple months came rushing back. "Damn him. Damn him and his selfish fucking ass."

Ray blew out a breath. "From what I found, their affair lasted two months. The day after Miller's doctor appointment confirming his pregnancy, your father broke things off with him."

"Fuck," Juan said, eyes closed.

"A friend of Miller's told me the omega thought a baby would make Jorge leave Eduardo. When it didn't, he was angry. They said he planned on forcing Jorge to pay child support and come clean to your papa."

"Why didn't he?" Juan asked. He felt so numb, as if he was hearing everything from a great distance away. He needed Jackson beside him.

"He met another man," Ray said. "His name was Oscar Mendez. From all accounts, the two fell in love."

"Why did he put my name on the birth certificate?" Juan asked, confused. "If he was going to lie, why not put his new man's name on it?"

"His friends didn't know," Ray said. "I spoke with his sister again, and she only told me that he thought you were a good man."

Juan rubbed his face. "He put my name there because my dad wouldn't step up."

"I think so," Ray said. "He got engaged to Mendez not long after Oscar was born. Then, about six months ago, the two were in a car accident. They both died almost immediately. Thankfully, Oscar was with Miller's sister."

"Then she called my dad." Juan nodded, picturing it all in his head. His dad would have answered right away, hoping Juan's papa wouldn't hear about it.

"I saw the phone records," Ray said. "She honestly thought you were the father. She asked for you, and your dad pretended to be you. He told her he wanted nothing to do with the baby."

Juan banged his head on the table. "What do I tell Papa?"

Ray sighed. "I don't know, Juan. Your dad is dead. There's no peace to be had from him. I suspect Eduardo knows something though. Your sister was right. He recognized Miller's name when Alex mentioned it."

Juan turned his face to look up at Ray. "What would you do?"

"I would talk to your papa and try to bring it up. See if he's receptive. If not, then try to forgive your dad and let it rest. If he is, then talk it out."

Juan sat up. "Okay. That's a plan."

He sat there, unable to get up.

"You're not like him," Ray said. "I would bet every dime I have in the bank that first, you would never cheat on your partner, and second, you would never abandon a child you helped create. You would have paid child support and tried your hardest to be a part of Oscar's life."

Juan stared at the table, wanting to believe Ray.

"Juan," Ray said, smacking the table. "Would you ever give Oscar up? Knowing he's not your son?"

Juan jerked back. "Hell no. Jackson and I are Oscar's daddies now. That's all there is to it."

"Then how can you possibly think you're like Jorge Vega? You are taking care of a child that's not even yours. You didn't fucking hesitate." Ray shook his head. "You are one of the best men I know. I will gladly remind you each time you start doubting that."

Juan felt a bit of the weight in his heart lift. "Thanks, Daddy."

Ray groaned, head falling back. "Get out of my house."

Juan grinned, feeling a lot better than when he'd arrived. "Love you too."

He said goodbye to all Ray's kids and pets, then headed toward his papa. It was Wednesday, so Juan's papa should still be home this early. Juan didn't think his book club met until after noon.

The small town was waking up, and traffic was as heavy as traffic in Hobson Hills got. The parking spots outside Zoe's bakery and Gib's diner were full, and people rushed toward the warmth within. Now that Christmas was over, the town was a little bare and the snow had taken over.

He parked his truck near the apartment complex and quickly jogged to his old door. He knocked once and his papa answered almost immediately.

Eduardo was still in his pajamas. He held the door open. "Juan? This is an early visit."

"I needed to talk to you." Juan stepped in and took

off his coat. The apartment was completely his papa's now. Juan had always loved the warmth of the kitchen back home in Arizona. It was the one room that Eduardo had controlled.

Now, his papa had his own home, and that warmth was everywhere from the row of potted cacti on the windowsill to the colorful rugs and fluffy throw pillows. He had decorated in wild, bold colors, and it all came together beautifully. Just like his papa. *How could Dad not treasure him?*

"Ray found out who Oscar's real alpha father was," Juan said, unable to hold it back anymore.

Eduardo closed his eyes and sighed. "Sit down. I'm getting some coffee."

Juan did as he was told and waited until his papa returned with two cups. He took one and sipped it while Eduardo got comfortable.

"I was very young when I met your dad," Eduardo said, eyes soft with fondness. "He was a handsome, charming man and promised that he'd treasure me forever. My parents weren't very affectionate, and I remember treasuring each casual touch he gave me. We'd hold hands, and he'd wrap his arm around my shoulders, and I'd feel like I belonged." Eduardo laughed and took a sip of his coffee. "I've talked a lot about things to Fawn, Min-Jun, and Clarice. They've helped me realize a few things. I was far too young to make the decision to marry Jorge. I was twenty, but I was so unprepared for marriage. It just seemed easier to do things the way he wanted, so slowly, I changed to be the traditional houseomega he wanted."

"I thought you were happy with him," Juan said softly.

Eduardo smiled. "I wasn't unhappy."

"That's not happiness," Juan said, frowning.

"No, it's not. Over the years, your father and I got along well enough, but our marriage wasn't like Gramps and Grammy's or John and Susan Benson's," Eduardo said.

"There are some strong couples in this town," Juan agreed.

"They give me hope," Eduardo said with a sad smile. "One of the things that *did* make me happy about my marriage to Jorge was the knowledge that he truly honored me as his husband. I had his faithfulness."

Juan wanted to cry. He didn't want to tell his papa that Jorge Vega had been a cheating bastard.

"The day he died, Jorge told me he had been unfaithful," Eduardo said, eyes filling with tears. "He told me he had slept with three other omegas while we were married. He mentioned a young omega named Lars and told me he had made so many mistakes."

"Papa," Juan said, moving to sit beside him. "I'm so sorry."

"Jorge dared to tell me that he wanted to clear the air between us for my sake." Eduardo laughed harshly. "Can you believe that? He said it was for *my* sake. As if I'm happier *knowing* he cheated on me."

"He did it to ease his own guilt," Juan said.

"Yes." Eduardo sighed, then took another sip of his coffee. "When that woman came in with Oscar and said the name Lars, I knew. I didn't want to know it, but I knew. You wouldn't have refused to take responsibility of your actions. Jorge would."

"I don't know what to say, Papa. How do I make this better?" Juan asked.

"You can't," Eduardo said. "What you can do is love Oscar as your own. I'm dealing with what happened. Moving here was the best thing I've ever done. Fawn and my other friends are exactly what I need. I can be myself here and deal with this emotional shit pile that Jorge left me. That's what Fawn calls it – an emotional shit pile."

Juan laughed roughly. "I'm here for you too, Papa. If you want to talk."

Eduardo leaned over and hugged him. "You are so different from your dad. You look just like him, but you are such a better person."

Juan squeezed his eyes shut. "Promise?"

"I swear it."

"Are you okay with Oscar?" Juan asked.

"In my mind, that little boy is *your* son, which makes him my grandson. I love him very much," Eduardo answered, patting his hand. "Don't think Oscar is some kind of symbol of Jorge's betrayal. I know he's just a little boy and has no blame in any of this."

"What should I tell Lucía?"

Eduardo sighed. "I'll be honest, but I don't want to have to talk about it."

"I'll call her and let her know." Juan nodded. "She suspected you knew, and she'll understand."

"Thank you," Eduardo said, sighing. "Now, I have to

get ready. Clarice has today off, so her and I are going shopping with Fawn. Not that I can afford any of the stores Fawn will want to go to, but it's fun to try the fancy things on."

Juan sat up and reached for his wallet. "Let me give you some money."

Eduardo held his hand out. "Absolutely not. Fawn tries to buy things for me all the time. I do *not* need any of those clothes. Trust me. I like gravy too much."

Juan hugged his papa one more time, then left. He drove straight to The Book Worm. Jackson was just opening it when Juan walked in.

Jackson's face lit up when he saw him. "Juan? Are you here to hug me?"

Juan pulled him into his arms and swung him around. "I love you so much, blue jay."

"Love you too, handsome. Now put me down before I puke on you."

CHAPTER 18

JACKSON - APRIL

Jackson reluctantly left Oscar with Ines and went to meet his friends for dinner. Juan had insisted Jackson needed a night out, especially since he was leading another Bigfoot excursion. Jackson had tried to tell him he had already found Bigfoot, but apparently, their dog didn't count.

Griff, Luke, and Britney sat at a back table at The Irish Rose. Griff was in his final trimester now, and his small baby bump had ballooned. Jackson swore it got bigger each day. Jackson's own baby bump was just now showing.

"Hey," Luke said, grinning. "I ordered fried pickles like you told me to."

Britney cooed and leaned over to kiss him. "You are such a good friend."

"He follows directions very well," Griff nodded. "We got Reuben's Fritters too."

Jackson pumped his fist. "Yes! Now, tell me how it's going."

Britney waved her hand in the air, fluttering her fingers. "Oh, nothing important happened recently. We're just –"

"Fuck me, that's a pretty diamond," Jackson said, grabbing her hand. "It's an engagement ring." He looked between her and Luke. "You guys are getting married?"

Britney grinned and nodded. "Yes! We're engaged. The wedding will be in the fall. I'm thinking October so both the babies will be born."

Jackson whooped and waved his arms in the air. "I'm so happy for you two."

Luke wrapped an arm around her shoulders. "It seemed the right time. My dealership is doing alright, and I think we'll turn a profit soon."

"Plus, I make good money, so we'll start saving for the wedding now." Britney bounced in her seat. "I can't wait to drag Luke to cake tastings."

"I'll buy your cake," Jackson said. "My gift to you guys."

Britney's lip trembled. "Really?"

"Yes," he said, nodding. "You two are my friends, and I love you."

"I'm paying for the venue," Griff said. "Well, as long as you'll have it on a Sunday at The Irish Rose."

Luke snickered. "So, you can get it from Justin for free?"

Griff laughed. "Of course."

Jackson squeezed his cheeks. He was so unbelievably happy. "I can't wait."

"We also decided on the name for the baby," Griff

said. They had discovered they were having a girl a while ago but couldn't agree on a name. "We're keeping it simple and naming her Rose."

Jackson's shoulders slumped. "Not Dolly?"

"No," Griff said, groaning. "Name your own kid Dolly."

"We don't know what we're having yet. We want to be surprised," Jackson said, pouting. "Dolly is a good name."

"Don't force your Dolly Parton love on me," Griff said, throwing a straw wrapper at him. "Oh, and Justin and Zed are driving me insane. They call every night to ask what I ate for dinner. They've even taught Bea to ask me what I've eaten that day as soon as she sees me." He eyed Jackson. "Now that I think about it, you do too."

"We love you," Jackson said, smiling sweetly. "At least Zed isn't trying to kill Luke now."

"Only because I protect him," Britney said, snickering. "He hides behind me each time Zed shows up."

"Which is *all* the time," Luke said, shuddering. "Why is your big brother so damn big?"

"It's that whole world he carries on his shoulders," Griff said, rolling his eyes. "I need to get him a pet. He spends way too much time alone worrying about me."

"What about you, Jackson?" Luke asked, leaning his arms on the table. "When are you and Juan tying the knot?"

Jackson froze, eyes blinking furiously. "Marriage?"

"You two live together, have a son, and are having a

baby soon," Luke said, looking at him like he was stupid. "That's the next step, right?"

"I never wanted to get married," Jackson said slowly, mind whirling.

"Oh," Griff said, sounding shocked. "I thought since you knew you trusted Juan, and you loved him, that you'd have moved past the whole fear of marriage thing."

"Is it your grandfather?" Britney asked nervously. "Is he still trying to make you marry men from his church?"

"He's *not* my grandfather," Jackson said automatically. "Gramps is my grandfather now. I have Grandpapa, Uncle John, and Aunt Susan. That's my papa's side of the family."

Her eyes softened. "I get it, hun."

"I have a restraining order too," Jackson said. "He's not allowed to contact me at all."

"So, no marriage?" Luke asked. "I guess it's still really early in your relationship. It makes sense to wait."

Jackson bit his lip. He already felt like he was married to Juan. His alpha was always there for him, and they fit together in a way Jackson had never thought possible. He knew Juan thought marriage was important, but he never complained about Jackson's hesitancy. He just let Jackson take the lead.

"I love Juan." Jackson frowned at the table. "Him and Oscar are my family."

"Okay," Griff said, nodding. "And?"

"And I want to marry him," Jackson said, eyes going wide. "Fuck nuggets! I want to marry Juan."

"Then you should ask him," Luke said. "We can plan a surprise, and, hey, where are you going?"

Jackson had stood and was looking around wildly. "I need to ask him. Now."

"Like, right this second?" Britney asked.

"Yes. He's at Reuben's cabin." Jackson started for the door right when the server brought their food.

"We need that to go," Luke yelled, standing and tossing cash on the table. "This is an emergency."

Griff scrambled from his chair and grabbed Jackson's arm. "Wait for us. I need to pee real quick."

Jackson groaned. "You guys are ruining the moment."

"I kinda have to pee too," Britney said. "Get me a soda to go, hun." She followed Griff.

About twenty minutes later, they all piled into Luke's car and started toward Reuben's cabin.

Griff passed him the box with the fritters, and Jackson got one out, dunking it in the secret sauce Reuben made.

"Don't drip shit on my seats," Luke said from up front.

Griff made a face and deepened his voice. "Don't drip shit on my precious tan leather seats. I love my car more than life itself."

Britney laughed and looked back toward them. "What are you going to say, Jackson?"

Jackson shrugged. "I don't know."

She pulled her phone up and started tapping on it. "I think poetry is a good start."

"Roses are red, violets are blue," Griff said.

"You have a nice ass, and I want to marry you," Luke finished.

"Not that kind of poetry," Britney said, rolling her eyes. "You two are ridiculous."

"I'd like to have my ass complimented some time," Luke said, grumbling. "A man likes to be appreciated."

"Aww, Luke, your ass is so firm and bouncy," Jackson said, making kissing faces. "It's just the cutest ass in the whole world."

"I hate you," Luke said. "Now what are you going to say?"

Griff pulled out a napkin. "Give me a pen. We'll figure this out."

By the time they got to Reuben's cabin, Jackson had a full speech written out on the napkin and had practiced it three times. "I got this."

"You so got this," Britney said and handed him one of her gold bangles. "It's not a ring, but you need something to give him. It's a symbol of infinite love."

"Uh, okay." Jackson took her bangle and stuck it in the pocket of his jacket. "Should we add that to the speech?"

"It's too late," Griff said. "We're here. Don't worry. You're going to do alright."

Jackson barely waited until Luke parked the car to open the door and jump out. Reuben had insisted that they had to stay in the cabin if they were going to spy on Bigfoot until Ernie had the baby which could be any day now.

He ran up the steps, and the door swung open.

Ray stood there, looking worried. "Jackson, what's wrong? You look upset."

"Gotta talk to Juan." He pushed past Ray, vaguely aware of his friends following him.

Juan sat at the table with Ernie and Mateo. They were studying three separate screens. "That had to be a rabbit," Matteo said in disappointment. "It had a white fluffy tail. Bigfoot doesn't have that."

"Juan," Jackson said, and his alpha jumped, looking up.

"Jackson? Blue jay, what's wrong."

"Marry me," Jackson yelled. "You're marrying me. I like your ass."

Griff groaned. "We had a speech written, Jackson. Damn it."

Jackson pulled the bangle from his pocket and thrust it at Juan. "You're mine. Forever."

Britney tsked. "Try a little less creepy and more romantic. It's a symbol of infinite love, remember?"

Juan seemed frozen for a moment, and Jackson wanted to die. He'd assumed too much. Then that damn smirk covered Juan's face. The smirk that had made Jackson fall in love with the bastard.

"Okay, blue jay. I'll marry you."

"And now I'm posting this on my social media account," Luke said, waving his phone. "I recorded your romantic moment. Do you want a copy?"

"There was a speech," Griff said sadly.

Ernie patted his shoulder. "Do you want to read it to us?"

"Yes," Griff said. "Ernie, you be Juan, and I'll be Jackson."

"I'm recording this too," Luke said, holding his phone back up.

Jackson didn't care. Juan was watching him with that look in his eyes. The one that told Jackson he was the most beautiful and captivating person in the world.

CHAPTER 19

JACKSON - CHRISTMAS EVE

Jackson admired his reflection. "Why have I never worn suspenders before?"

"Because you're a farm boy hipster, not a nerdy hipster," Yeo said. Jackson's brother was two months pregnant and ridiculously perky. He practically bounced around the room.

Dean stood with his back against the wall. Jackson watched his papa grin as he watched all his sons getting ready for the wedding. He looked so damn proud.

Jackson and Juan had decided to have a Christmas Eve wedding at one of Barry Wilson's event barns. Barry had handled all the decorations and the reception. Jackson and Juan had dipped into their savings to pay for the wedding, but they both wanted to do it up right. Barry, of course, had refused to accept payment for his part in it. The Wilsons claimed Jackson and his brothers as their own.

Luke and Griff stood behind him, grinning at him

in the mirror. "You really do look like a nerdy hipster," Griff said.

His friend had had a healthy baby girl a few months ago. Rose now had a head full of blond hair and a sweet disposition. Jackson didn't know where the hell she got it from. A few weeks before Rose was born, Ernie had given birth to a little alpha named Maury whose disposition was a bit grumpier.

Jackson's own little terror was sleeping in Grandpa Ray's arms. Dylan Julio Vega looked just like his alpha daddy, but he had Jackson's eyes. The past year had brought Jackson and his friends a few more babies, a few more couples, and a lot more pets.

He couldn't wait to see what the next year would bring.

Barry poked his head in the door. "I need the flower-tossers and ringbearers."

Bea clapped and stood with Oscar. "We get to toss flowers, Oscar."

"Like we practiced," Oscar said, face extremely serious. "We gots to cover a lot of ground."

They ran out the door, and Jackson held back his laugh.

Min pulled Jun up from where Jackson's youngest brother sat, playing with a stuffed horse. "It's time, Jun. We gotta carry the rings."

"Bring horsey," Jun said, frowning.

"Okay. I'll bring my fox," Min said and grabbed his stuffed fox. "We gotta get them married, Jun. Come on."

Jackson exchanged amused looks with his other

brothers. Min had finally started to like Jun. It had just taken two years.

Dean clapped his hands. "Okay, kids. Line up. Griff, you go first, then Luke, Yeo, Jimmy, Jake, and Jules. Remember not to rush down the aisle and follow Barry's directions."

"Yes, Papa," all of them said, including Griff and Luke.

"That's right," Dean said. "You'd best obey me. Now get moving."

The line moved out the door, leaving Dean with Jackson.

Dean took Jackson's hands and looked him over. Jackson wore tan slacks, a pink shirt, and red, white, and pink patterned suspenders. His hair was parted like it always was, and his freckles still covered his face. He was a little plumper from the pregnancy, but otherwise, Jackson was just Jackson.

"You are so handsome, baby boy," Dean said, eyes full of love. "I'm proud of you."

"For getting married? Don't tell Jimmy that, or he'll rush out and hunt someone down."

"No," Dean said, shaking his head. "I'm proud of you for working through your fears. I know seeing and living through your alpha father's rants was traumatic."

"He's not my father. Ray is," Jackson said, nodding. "I know a good person when I see them now."

Dean cupped his face. "That is why I'm proud of you. You're doing something I worried you would never want to do. Marriage isn't a perfect solution or situation for everyone, but it works for you and Juan."

"I love you, Papa," Jackson said. "You were brave too. Seeing that made me brave. I can do this. I know I can."

Dean kissed his forehead. "Someone wants to talk to you before you walk down the aisle." He opened the door and Gramps slipped in.

"Gramps." Jackson grinned. "I'm getting married."

The older man smiled softly. "That you are. I wanted to give you something, and I know you'll be distracted at the reception."

Jackson hugged him tightly. "A hug?"

"That too." Gramps chuckled. "I want you to know I signed the house over to you." Gramps kissed the top of his head when he gasped. "No arguing."

Jackson leaned back. "I can't accept that, Gramps. Juan and I almost have enough saved to pay market value for it. That's the plan."

Gramps squeezed his shoulders. "I know you wanted to buy it from me, but you're my grandson. This is what family does."

Jackson felt his eyes water. "Gramps."

"Now, I think you have an alpha waiting for you at the altar."

Jackson gave him a shaky smile. "He's a pretty patient man. He was a virgin, you know. He saved himself for me."

Dean snorted. "Sure he was, baby boy. Sure he was. Come on now."

They left the room and Jules waved at them before he took his turn down the aisle.

"How did Jules get so tall?" Jackson whispered.

"I have no idea," Dean said. "He's still as sweet as ever though. He doesn't stink as bad as Jake."

Jackson shuddered. "Teenagers."

Barry grinned and waved at them. "It's your turn."

Gramps went and wrapped his arms around his son and they both watched Jackson, identical grins on their faces.

A light and folksy violin solo filled the room, and Dean held his arm out. "Are you ready?"

"Hell yeah," Jackson said and took his papa's arm.

The open event barn was full of Wilsons and their other friends from Hobson Hills. Even a few of Juan, Ray, and Carter's army buddies had shown up for the occasion. For some reason, they were amused by Jackson's virginal alpha getting married.

His friends and family lined the right side of the altar, and Carter, Ray, Lucía, Ernie, Nico, and Mateo lined the left side. Juan looked damned fine in his suit. His green fauxhawk was grown out to the perfect length, and he was giving Jackson that look that made him shiver. *I love that alpha. Time to get married*

Juan

JUAN DANCED with Jackson to Dolly Parton's "Wildflowers." The reception was in full swing and the dancefloor was packed. Miss Mona and Bigfoot ran around the crowds, soaking in all the petting and pampering they were getting since they were the only pets there. Miss Mona looked particularly lovely with her wedding veil hairband.

His papa danced with Fawn and all their friends. Juan had never seen him look so happy. A year had brought him some measure of peace. Lucía spun around the floor with Manuel, reminding Juan of her wedding earlier in the year.

"Can I cut in?" Mrs. Odell asked, nudging Jackson aside without bothering to wait for an answer.

Jackson huffed. "Evil woman, I'm hunting down Doc Grover and dirty dancing with him."

"Take pictures," Mrs. Odell said and waved him away.

Juan laughed and spun her around the room. "Love you, lady."

"Love you too, Juan. I wanted to congratulate you. Rosemary and the other Dolly's Diamonds and Dragons will get around to it too."

"Thanks." Juan kissed her cheek. "Do you realize how much you and the others have helped me and Jackson?"

"As much as you two have helped us." Her smile lit up her wrinkled face. "We all carry our burdens, hot lips. I'm happy I could be here to watch you two work through your baggage. You made a cute kid too."

Juan looked to the side and saw Jackson holding Dylan in his arms. He watched the baby with wonder. "Yeah, we sure as shit did."

"I think Eduardo's song's coming up next. You better grab your papa." She spun him toward Eduardo and his group of friends as Dolly's "Love is like a Butterfly" began.

Juan grabbed his papa's hand. "Dance with me?"

Eduardo grinned. "Remember this song? You and me would dance around the kitchen."

Juan pulled him into his arms. "I do remember. I treasured those times, Papa. This song and those memories got me through some tough times."

Eduardo sniffed. "Damn it, but I'm proud of you."

"For getting married? It's not that hard."

"No," Eduardo said, rolling his eyes. "I'm proud of the man you are. Seeing you with Jackson and the children warms my heart. Seeing you with your friends makes me laugh. You're a funny, smart, and kind man. You're just plain good, Juan. I love you."

"I love you too, Papa." Juan pushed back his tears and enjoyed dancing with his papa.

A few hours later, they cut the gorgeous and tasty cake Reuben had created for them, and before he knew it, Juan was shoved into a sleigh with Jackson.

Harper's ponies whinnied a hello. They would be riding to Reuben's cabin for a one-night honeymoon. Christmas was tomorrow, and there was no way they were going to miss opening presents with Oscar.

Gramps looked over his shoulder. "Ready to slip away?"

Juan cupped Jackson's face, lost in his omega's green eyes. He couldn't resist dipping down and tasting his lips. *I love this man so much.*

"I'm gonna take that as a yes," Gramps said and whistled at the horses to start moving.

4. Healing the Omega – https://amzn.to/2FNcXrY
5. A Pint for my Omega – https://amzn.to/2XItQf7
6. Unraveling the Omega – https://amzn.to/2xRCnRL
7. The Alpha's Christmas Wish
8. Noah's story (Title to be determined) – *Coming Soon*

Hobson Hills Shorts – short stories from the world of Hobson Hills Omegas

1. The Beta's Love Song – https://amzn.to/2UrRPNN
2. Bennett's Dream – https://amzn.to/2GwSpG3
3. Justin's Journey – https://amzn.to/2DhW1t1
4. Grey's Gift – https://amzn.to/2BcjxXf
5. Hobson Hills Shorts: Volume One – https://amzn.to/2M3oGGZ

Holiday Omegas Shorts – holiday short stories from the world of The Silver Isles – paranormal, mpreg

1. Cauldron Cake Pops and a Witch's Kiss – https://amzn.to/33wMrhc
2. Sugar Cookies and a Witch's Love – *Coming December, 2019*
3. Candy Hearts and a Witch's Ring – *Coming in February, 2020*

The Silver Isles – paranormal, mermen, mpreg

1. The Guppy Prince – https://amzn.to/2q9Q8en
2. The Not so Little Merman – *Coming Soon*
3. The Sea Witch – *Coming Soon*

If you would like to keep up with releases, please like and follow me on Instagram (@c.w._gray) or Facebook (@cwgrayauthor), join C.W. Gray's Reading Nook on Facebook, or visit my website at https://cwgray-author.com.

Unedited excerpt from *The Mercenary's Mate* – Book One in the Blue Solace Series

Silverlight System, Planet Vextonar

"Next up is a real gem, gentle folks!" The auctioneer leered toward the large crowd at the bottom of the stage. He was a Betonize-human hybrid, sharp teeth a glaring white. "This little girl's part Prime and part Lower. Don't see that on Vextonar too often."

The crowd's boisterous laughter and cheering filled the room. Eight people had already been auctioned off, and the day was still young. Leti Ando gritted his teeth and awkwardly shuffled his feet. The bulky cast on his lower leg made him slower than normal, and there were too many strangers here, too much movement. He wanted to be in his rooms, reading the new Old-Earth journal he'd gotten his hands on.

Draif shot him a sympathetic look. Leti's best friend

was no less uncomfortable in the auction house but had insisted on coming with him. "You knew it'd be like this, Master," Draif whispered.

Leti glared at his friend, his black eye and busted lip protesting the expression. "I hate it when you call me that."

Draif gave him a small smile, dark eyes on the stage. "I know. Why do you think I do it?" His smile faded. "It's her, Leti."

Leti startled, stumbling and knocking into some of the men around him. He did his best to ignore the grumbles, his heart beating fast in his chest. Monty slipped from his head to his shoulder, and Draif grabbed his arm to steady him. For such a small, slender man, Draif had a strong and sure grip that came in handy when Leti's clumsiness attacked.

Leti ignored the grumbles around him, eyes locked on the stage. A modestly dressed woman stood tall. She held a whimpering, blanket-wrapped bundle in her arms.

"This little lady is up for sale," the Auctioneer said. "She comes from a Prime daddy and his mistress, a Lower woman. Unnamed infant, but good potential. Mommy's dead and Daddy don't want a Lower brat, so there won't be no contest of ownership once she's bought. We'll start bidding at 250? Can I get 250?"

Leti sighed and closed his eyes. "I can't believe Father is selling his own child. I hate that he deals in slavery at all, but his own daughter?"

"Yeah, well, he didn't seem to like your opinion too much last night when you brought it up." Draif grabbed his hand and squeezed. "Not that he needs much excuse to beat the shit out of you. It was the threat to sell you too that worries me the most."

It wasn't appropriate for a bed-slave to hold his master's hand, but the two of them had never been *appropriate*. Nothing was normal about a Prime citizen who didn't have sex with his bed-slave, little less treat him like a slave, and nothing was normal about a bed-slave who was demisexual and had a scarred face and damn good fighting skills.

Draif had been Leti's best friend since they were both fifteen. Leti's father gave him to his son and told him to dominate the "broken" slave and prove himself a man. The arrogant Prime often told his son that he was so fat and awkward that no one would ever want him, especially with his attention always on his studies and research.

Leti might be a breeder male, able to have children, but his father assured him no one would ever offer for him like they would a daughter. And love? According to his father, no one could ever love him, not even some mixed breed alien. Being a breeder male showed his blood was too diluted to be human enough. There was too much Wello blood in his ancestry. Father always blamed Leti's mother for it, but never to her face. He was an arrogant bully, not stupid.

In his father's mind, a bed-slave would guarantee that Leti would at least be a man in the bedroom. Leti tried not to complain too much, though. Draif had proven to be the best thing that ever happened to him. He was his loyal confidant and best friend from the start and soon became his assistant, body guard, and overall jack-of-all-trades.

Where Leti struggled in anything outside of his books and pets, Draif could seemingly master any skill if he set his mind to it. More importantly, though, Leti loved Draif more than anything in all the galaxies. He was his brother in all but blood. His family.

"620 to the Drall in the corner. Can I get 630, anyone? 630?"

"Is your lawyer bidding?" Draif whispered.

Leti looked at his communicator. "Yes. He'll keep topping whatever's offered. She'll be ours in a few minutes."

"You father won't like that, Leti. What are we going to do? We can't hide her in your rooms until she's eighteen. I guess we could put her in Wobble's stable, but who wants to live with an Old-Earth Llama?" Draif paused and eyed his friend. "Well, except for you."

Leti grinned. "When I get her, you are going to take her to the spaceport. Talk with Dottie. She's going to sneak all of us on a random ship going out of the system. Father would be alerted if we used our passports, so we have to sneak, at least at first. Once we're out of the Silverlight system, I can tear up your contract as well as hers. You'll both be free."

Draif squeezed his hand tight. His eyes left the stage, widened in disbelief. "We're leaving the system?"

Leti snorted. "I've given you several chances to leave over the last ten years, but you wouldn't go."

"I couldn't possibly leave you behind. I love you," he said with no hesitancy. "What about your menagerie?"

Draif looked at the vexal newt happily perched on Leti's shoulder. "Monty here wouldn't be a problem, but you can't possibly expect to sneak all of them onboard a ship and I know you won't leave them." Draif shook his head, dumbfounded. "What about money? How will you survive? I can easily get work, but you're a trained historian. They aren't exactly rolling in credits." He paused, already forming a plan. "I could work and you could stay home and take care of the baby. You'd be good at that. You love. It's your thing, and in the end, that's all it really takes. We can figure out how to feed her and change a diaper."

"1050! Can I get 1100? Anyone? 1100?"

"Dottie assures me it will be fine. She's picked out a Drellian cargo vessel and my pets are heading there as we speak, even Wobble." Leti checked his comm, then continued, "As for money, I've been saving for a long time. Do you really think I spend all the credits Father gives me monthly?"

"He's always complaining that you drain his pocket, but I thought he was just being cheap. All you buy are books on your tablet, presents for me, and things for the pets. I think the most expensive thing you bought was the tablet. It came from the Anchor's Rest System, right? Our system is seriously behind on tech."

Leti nodded. "I don't usually use more than a quarter of the allowance. I've been saving my pay from my publications too. It's certainly not much, but I didn't become a historian to make money. I never thought I'd have to." Leti laughed ruefully. "I'm a privileged Prime, right?"

Draif let go of his hand and smacked his arm. "No self-deprecation allowed! We are who we are, there's no changing that. Especially on this world. It's not like you can change castes and become a Worker. Anyways, the gods know that no one deserves to be related to your father or psycho mother." He smiled sadly and nodded toward Leti's broken ankle. "Their love hurts."

Draif looked worried. "Are you going to pack and bring my things too?"

"Of course! Melinda has already started packing for us."

"Will she alert your father?"

Leti checked his comm again. Things were on track. "No. She's the one who urged me to start saving credits when I was twelve. Once we leave, she's going to go to Rothwell and work with her daughter."

"Good." Draif's couldn't seem to stop smiling. "We're really doing this?"

"1520 to the gentleman at the front! 1600 anyone? 1600? Going once. Going twice. Sold to the gentleman in the blue coat!"

Despite his worry, Leti grinned. "Yes. We're really doing this."

Buy Here: My Book

EXCERPT

EXCERPT

Excerpt from *The Guppy Prince*, book one in The Silver Isles.

Dover Rees floated in the deepest part of his creek, enjoying the rushing sound of the waterfall to his right. Sunlight filtered through the water, glinting off the deep blue of his guppy tail. His thin and delicate caudal fin spread out like an elegant fan, dancing through the warm water as he swayed.

His favorite smooth and colorful pebbles were strewn around below him, and he admired the shells he had collected and placed beside them. Dover breathed deeply and enjoyed the peace and quiet. No one mocked him or bossed him around. No one watched him with cold eyes and hidden smirks. *I wish I could stay here forever.*

Sudden movement beside him jarred him from his thoughts and he laughed when Chubber grabbed a bright pink stone in his small brown paws and swam away. Dover's otter friend liked to steal Dover's shinies then share them with him again later.

A brook trout swam past him and Dover debated grabbing it for an early lunch, but he wasn't too hungry yet. Lately, he'd been eating less and less, and he couldn't make himself care.

The quiet water around him hummed as Nami quickly swam to him. His best friend's guppy tail was a lovely pink pattern with black dots, and her short black hair floated around her head. The cat with a mermaid tail on her black tankini top made him smile. He loved her purr-maid shirts.

"Have you eaten today, Your Highness?" she asked.

Dover scowled. "Don't call me that."

"When you're acting like a pouting asswipe, that's what you get called." Nami wrapped her arms around him and settled her head on his shoulder. "What's wrong with you, Dover?"

Dover had no answer for her. All he knew was he felt empty inside and it was harder and harder to get up in the morning. "I think I ate some bad clams."

"Every day for the past two months?" Nami leaned back and glared at him, her dark eyes seeing right through him.

Chubber came to his rescue, swimming in between them and wrapping his lean body across Dover's shoulders. "Chubber wants to get a snack."

Nami sighed, bubbles filling the water around her. "Mom is in your cottage making lunch. You're worrying us, bluetail."

Dover stroked a hand through her hair, then shoved

her down and pushed up, swimming toward the surface.

"Damn it!" Nami swam after him.

He laughed, heart warming. *Someone cares about me.* It wasn't his family, but Nami and her mom were closer to him than his parents or any of his twelve siblings.

Chubber clung to his back and nibbled on his ear until he mentally apologized. Chubber cared about him the most.

His creek was deep, but it didn't take him long to reach the surface. Shauna waited for them on the shore, hands on her hips. Chubber's mother, Shell, stood on her hind legs beside the mermaid, chirping loudly. Uh oh. He really was in trouble.

"You didn't eat breakfast, did you?" The wind blew strands of Shauna's pink hair across her face, ruining her glare.

"Sorry, Shauna."

She sighed. "I made your favorite."

"Grilled shrimp salad?" Dover's stomach rumbled.

"With avocado, papaya, mango, and pineapple. All your favorites." Shauna gave him a soft look. "Come eat, bluetail."

Dover summoned his human legs and a few seconds later, walked out of the creek, naked, with Chubber clinging to his shoulder. Shauna handed him a deep teal sarong, and he tied it about his waist.

Shell crawled up his leg and into his arms, then rubbed her slick furry face against his. She was a bit heavier than Chubber, but he was still a baby.

"Why does he get all the loving?" Nami asked, grumbling as she tied a sarong around her own waist.

Dover chuckled when Shauna arched an eyebrow at her daughter. "Did you say something, sweetness?"

"No, ma'am," Nami said, wincing.

"You two come eat lunch." Shauna turned around and walked toward Dover's large cottage.

Dover closed his eyes for a moment and savored the feel of the moss-covered rocks under his feet, and the comfortable breeze quickly drying his curly blue hair. He loved his home so much. It was his sanctuary.

Buy Here: https://amzn.to/2q9Q8en